Lorie's cell phone rang.

Lorie checked the display, then looked at Matt. "I don't know who this is."

Matt flipped open the phone and hit the answer button, putting it on speaker.

"You have been a very naughty girl, haven't you, going to the law like that. Shame on you." The robot-processed voice was back.

Lorie turned pale. Matt put a finger to his lips.

"But then you know that, don't you? I'm surprised at you, trusting a deputy. When he finds out the truth, you'll finally be accountable."

Combined with the call Gerhardt had fielded, all Matt's dark suspicions came flooding back. *Was* she responsible for more than justifiable homicide? Lorie's expression held no hint of guilt, just confusion and fear.

"Why are you tormenting me?" Lorie demanded. "What did I ever do to you?"

"Why, you killed Grayson, of course. You have to be punished for that, since the court let you go. You'll finally get what you deserve. I hope your life insurance is up-to-date."

MARION FAITH LAIRD

shares a house with her mom and a gazillion books. She plays assorted musical instruments, including the organ at her church, composes and arranges music, sings, acts, and occasionally indulges in artwork. She's always had characters running around in her brain, and is glad she has a new way to share them with others.

In addition to the arts, Marion loves making things. She'd time-travel to the Renaissance if she could to study art technique, but she'd always come back home for her computer.

Growing up in a navy family, Marion has lived from one end of the U.S. to the other, and changed schools and curricula like some kids change shoes. Her peripatetic upbringing has given her a lifelong love of travel and learning, as well as awareness that while people's customs may differ, their hearts are the same.

Marion is a member of Romance Writers of America and American Christian Fiction Writers.

No Place to Run
Marion Faith Laird

HARLEQUIN® LOVE INSPIRED® SUSPENSE

Recycling programs
for this product may
not exist in your area.

™ LOVE INSPIRED BOOKS

ISBN-13: 978-0-373-44605-6

NO PLACE TO RUN

Copyright © 2014 by Marion Faith Laird

www.Harlequin.com

Printed in U.S.A.

Peace I leave with you, my peace I give unto you: not as the world giveth, give I unto you. Let not your heart be troubled, neither let it be afraid.

—*John* 14:27

For Mom, who inspired me to read because she always was, and to write because she wrote and told amazing stories! I'm glad she's here to read this.

And for Dad, who always encouraged me to follow my dreams. I wish he could hold a copy of this book, but I'm sure he knows.

Acknowledgments

Special thanks to my friend Anne, who introduced me to Love Inspired books back when they were Steeple Hill. I believe I can safely say that if it wasn't for her, this book wouldn't have been written. She'll always have a special place in our hearts' albums.

I'm indebted to the generous writers who helped me fine-tune my first chapter and cover blurb entry in Harlequin/Mills & Boon's annual So You Think You Can Write contest, especially Laura Hamby, Valerie Parv, Rachel J. Stevens and Kathi Robb Harris. I also thank Danica Favorite, who assured me that the editors would contact anyone whose work they wanted to see, even if the manuscript didn't make it past the first round of voting. Many thanks to Tina James, who requested the full manuscript and a synopsis, Lynette Eason, who helped me improve my synopsis, and to Elizabeth Mazer, my editor, who called and bought the book! Through the revision process, she's helped make it so much better than it was in its beginning!

Thanks also to Cheryl Wyatt. I've started many a story from her writing challenges (although not this one). I also appreciate the writing challenges on the Community Boards at Harlequin, and the interactive novel writing at PanHistoria.com. It's been said it takes a village to raise a child. I'm beginning to think it takes a village to nurture a writer! Many thanks to all my "villages," and to more of my "villagers," (in alphabetical order) Diana Cosby, Margaret Daley, Nell Dixon, Rachelle McCalla, Shirlee McCoy, Camy Tang and Janet Tronstad.

ONE

The note was unsigned.

Don't think you can get away with it.

The computer printout lay on the pile of library in-mail, as innocent as a rattlesnake ready to strike. Lorie stared at the words for one frozen moment as her heart began to race. She couldn't hear. Couldn't see anything except the note.

This couldn't be happening.

Not now.

Not after her prayers had been answered to let her begin rebuilding her life in Dainger County.

By the time the other librarian, Jen Burkhalter, loped into the office and slung her denim purse onto the coatrack, Lorie was shivering.

"The weather's gorgeous. I think spring decided to stick around a little longer." Jen's head jerked in a double take, her short black hair quivering. "What's wrong? Are you cold? You look like a deer in headlights."

Lorie sent a silent prayer heavenward. *Help!* Taking a deep breath to calm herself, she shook her head. "I'm fine."

Jen stuck her fists on her generous hips. "Don't try to put one over on a mom. If you're fine, I'm a sunflower in a cornfield. Now what's the problem?"

It took a moment for Lorie to calm down sufficiently to speak. "Have you heard any talk about my moving back to town?"

Jen looked surprised. "You mean trash talk? No. Why?"

You can do this. Taking a deep breath for courage, Lorie nodded at the note. "Look at the in-box. Somebody doesn't want me here."

Jen peered into the in-box, adjusting gold wire-rim glasses. "Oh, my. Get away with what?"

Murder.

But it wasn't.

An icy shiver of doubt skittered up Lorie's spine. What if someone thought it was?

Get a hold of yourself. This isn't San Diego.

Lorie pulled herself together. "Maybe they left it on the wrong desk."

"With your name on it?" Jen jerked her thumb in the direction of Lorie's Head Librarian plaque. "Stop grasping at straws. Everybody knows who the new head librarian is. You haven't touched the paper, have you?"

Lorie shook her head. "I've read enough mysteries to know that's the worst thing I could do."

"Then you also know we need to call the sheriff's department."

Call the law? Fear stabbed Lorie in the gut. "But what if this is just a prank?"

"What if it isn't?"

Lorie winced.

"Grimace all you want to, but if you don't call them, I'm going to."

"All right." Lorie's sigh ruffled the papers on her desk. "We'd better use the phone at the main desk, in case there are fingerprints."

"Good idea." Jen followed Lorie out the door, closing it after them, the automatic lock clicking into place.

As she reached for the phone at the circulation desk,

Lorie's stomach roiled. *Lord, why me?* If she never had to talk with another person in law enforcement, it would still be too soon.

You can do this. Her inner pep talk wasn't working. *You have to.*

She glanced back at Jen. "What's the phone number?"

"You could just dial 911."

"It isn't an emergency. It's just a—" What *was* it exactly?

"A personal threat." Jen finished the thought for her. "Something you can't afford to take lightly."

"You don't know the phone number, do you?"

"Here." Jen punched in seven digits and shoved the beige receiver at Lorie.

"Dainger County Sheriff's Department."

The receptionist's voice was warm, honeyed and very Southern. She also sounded vaguely familiar, but Lorie couldn't put a name to the voice. Just hearing the words "Sheriff's Department," Lorie swallowed hard and almost hung up. Jen, noticing her hesitation, glared at her.

Lorie cleared her throat. "This is Lorie Narramore at the county library. I'd like to report an incident." There. She'd said it, as if the note were the only thing wrong.

"Why, Loretta Lee, is that you?"

Lorie rolled her eyes. A few years in California had eliminated Loretta Lee from her name. A few minutes in Daingerville brought the ponderous moniker back.

"Yes, it is."

"This is Vangie Rae Sutherland. Used to be Vangie Rae McCormick, remember?"

Could she ever forget her old school nemesis? "It's nice to hear your voice again, Vangie." The Lord would forgive her for exaggerating. She hoped.

"Goodness gracious, I haven't seen you in forever!" Vangie sounded delighted. "I'd heard you'd moved back. You're at the county library, you said?"

"Mmm-hmm." *Reduced to wordless sounds? Really, Lorie, you're a grown-up. You shouldn't let her do this to you.*

"That explains why we haven't run into each other, then. Frank and I always go to the city library in West Bluff. How do you like being back here with your family?"

The unbusinesslike tenor of the conversation gave Lorie a headache, but she answered automatically.

"It's been fine…" Lorie caught Jen's Momzilla *I'll get you if you don't 'fess up right this second* face. "Look, when I went into my office just now, I found a threatening note on my desk."

"Ooh, that sounds serious." The threat might sound serious, but Vangie sure didn't. A clicking sound issued from the phone speaker, as if Vangie were making a note on her computer. "Are you still single?"

"What?" The sudden change of subject sent Lorie's brain reeling. What could her marital status possibly have to do with the case? If there *was* a case…

"We have several good-looking deputies I've been trying to match up with someone, but—"

Fear morphed into irritation. "Vangie, it doesn't matter. There's a threatening note on my desk."

"Well, of course it matters. If you're not divorced or anything, I've got a couple of good Christian boys I could send out."

Lorie sighed. Vangie Rae must not have outgrown her high-school matchmaking tendencies. *Lord, preserve me!*

"I'm not divorced. I've just been too busy to get married." *Not to mention getting dumped twice by guys I should have known better than to date in the first place. And—* No. Lorie refused to dwell on the main reason she hadn't had a husband or at least a fiancé when she'd left the West.

"Good." A few clicks issued from the line. "Now, tell me what this note said."

"Something like, 'You won't get away with it.'"

More clicking sounded on the other end of the line. "Can't you see it?"

"No. I left it in the office. I'm calling from the checkout desk."

"Oh, very good. It'll be better if you haven't got fingerprints all over the place."

Yanking her attention back from the computer, Lorie switched the phone to her other ear. "We all share the office, so my prints are probably on everything except the note. At least, they shouldn't be on it, unless the person responsible used my printer paper."

"Now, now, don't go looking on the gloomy side, Loretta Lee." She still pronounced Lorie's first name as though it were two words: Lo Retta, emphasis on the Lo. "We've already alerted one of our deputies."

"Thanks, Vangie." There was no sense in taking her frustration out on her old school frenemy. Getting on the wrong side of Vangie Rae had always had dire consequences, even before she was in law enforcement. "I never dreamed you'd grow up to work at the sheriff's office."

"Neither did I, but then I met Frank, and my entire career plans changed."

Frank Sutherland. The Dainger County Sheriff. Duh. Vangie was Mrs. Lawman-in-Chief. Suddenly everything made sense. Vangie was bubbly enough to make the station a friendlier place. With her at the reception desk, crime in Dainger County had probably plummeted to an all-time low.

Until someone decided to threaten the new head librarian...

"Let's see now. We have several single deputies, and I've put in a request for—"

"Vangie, I'm not angling for a date." Lorie fought down her irritation. *Especially not a deputy!* "I just want to find out who sent the note and stop them from sending any more." There. At least she *sounded* calm.

"Are you sure? Because after the men you probably dated in California, the fellows here are gonna be a whole lot more real."

That's right, Vangie. Diss the place where I'd still be living if my world hadn't collapsed.

Beeping noises issued from the receiver.

"I have more calls coming in. One of our more eligible deputies should be there within an hour, unless there's an emergency. I surely am glad to talk to you again, Loretta. We'll have to get together real soon, okay? Bye now!"

Vangie disconnected. Lorie stared at the receiver for a moment before replacing it on the cradle.

"So?" Jen sounded like an overeager reporter.

"Vangie Rae." Lorie rolled her eyes. "Why didn't you warn me?"

Jen straightened the free bookmark dump. "I didn't know you knew the Sutherlands."

"I've only met the sheriff in passing, but I had several classes with Vangie. Now she's threatening to set me up with one of the deputies. The last thing I have time for is a romance." *With a lawman, especially.*

Jen clucked her tongue. "Honey, everybody needs love in their life." Jen started straightening the brochures in the Summer Reading Program display.

Could her day *get* any worse? "I didn't say I didn't need love. I just don't need romance."

Jen shrugged. "Keep on believing that if you want to. Time to open the doors." She took the library keys from her pocket and ambled toward the entrance.

As Lorie got to work, hushed voices discussing the latest offerings on the new-books shelf trickled through the inside return slot. The coiled spring wound around her insides relaxed. At least she was doing one thing right.

After checking in the returned books and arranging

them on their respective shelves, Lorie returned to the office. The impulse to check the door to make certain it was locked almost overwhelmed her, but she squashed it, hoping she and Jen hadn't already destroyed fingerprint evidence on the handle.

"Ms. Narramore?"

Lorie started, turned and collided with a solid mass of muscle in a tan uniform. A crackle of electricity jolted her. Was it that dry in here?

"Oh, I'm sorry."

"Dispatch sent me. Threatening note?" The voice issuing from the strong face was a warm baritone.

Lorie met his incredibly blue eyes, shaded by a fawn Stetson. *Whew. Okay. Calm down. This is the investigating officer.* Without meaning to, she checked his left ring finger. Bare. *It's none of your business. He's the law.*

Lorie cleared her throat. "Yes. It's right here, Deputy—" she glanced at his name tag "—MacGregor." Oh, my. Was this the MacGregor boy who'd been the top defensive linebacker for the Daingerville Diamondbacks when she was a lowly freshman? Glancing again at his face confirmed her suspicion. This had to be either Matt or one of his equally handsome brothers.

As Lorie started to insert the key into the lock, the door swung open of its own accord.

"What—"

"Don't touch it." Deputy MacGregor drew his sidearm and clicked off the safety as he motioned her away.

Lorie's heart threatened to stop. They *had* locked the door…hadn't they?

"Hands up in there. Sheriff's department." Deputy Mac-Gregor kicked open the office door and scanned the room for intruders.

It was empty.

He glanced over his shoulder at Lorie. "Is there another exit?"

"Just the window in the bathroom, but it's a little small.... Although they assured me it does meet fire safety standards—"

Deputy MacGregor had already moved to the door leading to the minuscule restroom. He nudged it with the toe of his shiny black work boot.

A breeze fluttered through the open casement and into the office, riffling through the papers on the desk.

"Was the window open when you arrived?"

Lorie shook her head. "I don't think so—but I didn't really think to look."

He took a step into the tiny space, enough to bring him close to the frame inset with frosted glass. Examining it, the deputy frowned.

"Screen's been sliced open." The deputy poked at it and then peered at the area around the lock. "Window's been jimmied."

Lorie could hardly hear him over the pounding in her ears. The harassment was starting again, and this time, she had no place to run.

"Wow, look at those scratches!"

Jen's voice made Lorie jump, as she hadn't heard her approach. Lorie glanced at Jen's feet. She *would* be wearing silent-soled cross-trainers today of all days.

"You didn't notice the window before?"

Lorie shook her head. "We keep that door shut most of the time." Maybe whoever had left the note had still been inside the bathroom while she was in the office.... Panic welled up inside her, but she managed to swallow the scream.

"And you're certain you locked the office door?" Deputy MacGregor sounded as if he wanted to get the whole picture.

Lorie shook her head, wishing she had a glass of water. Her mouth had gone completely dry. The proximity of the attractive deputy was not helping, either. "No, I'm not completely sure. I meant to, but I was pretty rattled. I might have forgotten."

"I locked it." Jen put her hands on her hips again. "I felt it catch."

"Right. Let's see the note."

Lorie moved to the desk and waved a hand at the in-box. "It's right—wait a minute."

"Is something wrong?"

No. Where was it? "The note. It isn't here."

"Come again?" Deputy MacGregor's sharp tone could have sliced through granite.

Lorie faced his unbelieving stare head-on.

"S-someone must have taken it."

Great. Just great. Matt's day was complete. First the lead on the meth-lab investigation dried up, and now this. Missing evidence.

Matt clicked the safety on and shoved his silver Colt 1991 back into the holster with unnecessary force.

"Where was it?"

"Right there." Lorie waved a pale, fine-boned hand over the in-box. "On top. It looked like a computer printout."

"Laser, ink-jet, dot matrix?"

"Ink-jet, I think. Full color, anyway. The letters were a deep tomato-red." Her voice wavered almost imperceptibly.

Matt took out his incident notebook and scrawled the information. "And it said…?"

"Something like 'You won't get away with it.'"

Jen piped up, "'Don't think you can get away with it.'"

Matt wondered whether Jen knew more about the note than she'd told Lorie. She was practically another sister to him ever since she'd married his best friend, but Matt had known her since her prankster days in junior high. Was this another one of her stunts? Matt fixed Jen with his best law-enforcement stare.

"And you know this because…?"

Jen sniffed. "I pay attention. And don't think this is some sort of 'let's fix Matt up with the new librarian' scheme Vangie Sutherland and I cooked up. Because it isn't."

Matt took stock of his old friend. According to J.T., she had stopped pulling pranks on people, but Matt wouldn't put writing a mysterious note as a joke past her. Still, actually threatening someone who seemed to be her friend was unlikely. And besides, she wouldn't be dumb enough to damage library property for a joke. Jen would never commit even a misdemeanor unless she'd lost her mind in the past few weeks.

Lorie appeared to be having her own doubts. Having been three grades ahead of her, Matt hadn't really known Lorie when he was growing up. She'd been one of the brainy kids, scrawny, with braces. Looked as though she'd turned out well, except for her lack of color. Closer inspection indicated her pallor hadn't come from makeup. Whether the note was legit or not, she was frightened.

"Jen couldn't have moved the note." Lorie's voice had grown steadier. "She's been with me since I spotted the note. And you saw the window."

Matt's old classmate nodded gravely, but she had a "so there" twinkle in her eye. This might have started as a serious call, but, from the look of things, Jen intended to go along with Vangie's eternal attempts at matchmaking. No way he'd put up with that. He'd phone J.T. and then drop by the house after work.

Matt tucked the notebook back into his pocket and turned to go.

"Aren't you going to dust for prints?" Lorie sounded disappointed. More, still frightened.

Matt looked back at Lorie. "On my way to the unit now for the kit. Be right back."

He headed out the door to Unit 5 and took a moment to

radio in a report. "Dispatch, this is MacGregor. Looks like a B and E at the library. I'm processing the scene now."

"Ten-four, Unit 5."

Snagging the fingerprint kit, Matt headed back toward the library. Detouring by the bathroom window, he scanned the vicinity for footprints. Nothing showed on the concrete. Little chips of metal scraped when the window had been jimmied were the sole physical evidence.

Matt frowned. The perp knew enough to be careful. That boded ill for the investigation. Very ill, indeed.

TWO

When Matt returned to the library office, Jen and Lorie were tampering with the scene.

"Hey! What do you think you're doing?" Their mad scramble through papers made the answer obvious. He had to stop them before they accidentally destroyed more evidence.

"Trying to find the note." Lorie sounded as though she were attempting to cover fear with defiance. Somehow he had to convince her he wasn't the enemy.

Her voice had that California crispness which years of watching television had led him to expect. She didn't sound like an Arkansan anymore. Matt wondered how long it would take her to get her accent back. Not that any-body local *had* an accent.... It was people in other areas.

Matt smiled at the thought, and Lorie returned it, this time minus the fear. Hello. Really great smile... Looking into her eyes like this, he hadn't expected to feel a bolt of attraction. Judging from the surprised expression on her face, he hadn't been the only one.

"Is this it?" Jen reached behind the potted sago palm in the corner. "Ouch. I always forget how scratchy that thing is."

She stood up, bringing a sheet of paper with her. Glancing at it, Jen blanched. "Oh. No. This isn't it."

"What did you find?" Lorie sounded hopeful.

"It isn't important." Jen crumpled it up and started to stuff it into a pocket.

Matt held out his hand. He kept it extended, giving her one of his looks until she put the now-wrinkled printout into his outstretched palm.

The paper was an invoice for new books. Only Jen's attempt to hide it made it suspicious. One more thing to add to his list of questions for later. After a cursory inspection, he handed it back. Jen squashed it into her pocket.

"I'll need you two to clear out while I dust the office."

Jen chuckled. "Wish you'd sweep while you're here."

"Jen, come on." Instead of sounding amused, Lorie's voice held a tremor.

Matt encompassed them both in a look as they moved away from the desks. "Don't leave the library. I'll call you when I'm done."

Lorie practically shoved Jen out the door and left him to his solitary task. Outside, people moved around. Library business as usual.

Matt frowned as he dusted the in-box on the head librarian's desk. Why would anybody threaten someone like Lorie Narramore? She seemed an unlikely target. Of course, you could never tell. Anyone could have secrets.

Matt finished gathering the prints, concentrating on the job at hand so fully that Lorie's sigh startled him. He looked up to find her at the door.

"Sorry this is taking so long."

Her answering smile was wan. "It takes as much time as it takes."

Matt grinned, trying to make her feel better. "Most civilians don't get that."

"I'm not most civilians."

Why did she look so sad when she said that? There was more to Lorie Narramore than met the eye. Although, despite trying not to notice, he liked the parts that did meet the eye.

"I'll need to print you and Jen, too, to eliminate yours."

Fear flashed in Lorie's eyes. Hmm. Why?

After a moment, Lorie nodded. "All right. I guess I'd forgotten that part."

Forgotten? Interesting.

"No need to be afraid. It doesn't hurt, you know."

"I know. It's just… Never mind."

She knew? Matt looked into her eyes more deeply, as if he'd be able to see what was troubling her. She looked as though she felt…guilty.

"I'll just get Jen." Lorie whirled and was gone before Matt could stop her. The idea of being fingerprinted seemed to alarm her way more than it should. He'd definitely have to do a background check on her the minute he was back at his office computer.

As Jen walked through the door, she was already speaking. "Do mine first. We have two patrons ready to check out." She held out both hands in a parody of arrests in old police movies.

Matt grinned as he quickly took Jen's prints, teasing and joking with her all the while. When he was done, Jen walked out the office door and Lorie came back in, hesitation in every step.

Odd. He could think of only one reason why she'd be so uneasy.

"You aren't just pulling my leg with this note business, are you?"

"No."

Lorie Narramore might not have written the note, but she felt guilty about something. He'd been in law enforcement long enough to recognize the signs. This situation was making her extremely uncomfortable, and Matt itched to know the reason why. Of course, he could just wait and run her prints. That would bring anything up through the system.

Why was he sure he'd find her there? And why did the thought bother him so much?

* * *

Lorie could almost see the wheels turning in Matt's brain. She hated the thought of telling him, but surely she didn't have to confess the whole, sordid story. Maybe she could get by with the least possible amount and still tell the truth.

"I was arrested once." The words left Lorie's lips before she could stop them. When was she going to learn how to keep her mouth shut?

Caution mingled with curiosity in those intense blue eyes of his. "For?"

Lorie took a deep breath. "Murder."

To do him credit, his expression grew concerned. "I'm assuming you were released or acquitted, or you wouldn't be standing here now."

"You don't have to tell me how blessed I was not to have been convicted, because I know. Even the thought of county lockup scares me silly." She plucked at her light blue shirtsleeves, twisting them, just barely conscious of the action but unable to stop.

The deputy's expression grew serious. "The note— 'Don't think you can get away with it'—you think it's referring to what happened?"

"It could. I don't know." Lorie bit her lip. "After the trial and the publicity, doing my job at home became impossible. Then the harassment started. Notes, like this. Anonymous phone calls. It went on for months. When my family told me there was an opening for head librarian here, I jumped at it."

"Does the board know?"

Lorie nodded. "I had to give them full disclosure. It was only right, in case the bad publicity followed me. Thankfully, they decided to take a chance on me, in spite of attempts by some to quash the deal. I'm determined not to let the county down. Or my fellow librarians, either. They've stood by me from the first. They don't even think about it anymore. Only now…"

"Only now someone is making life difficult for you here."

Lacing her fingers calmed her. "If only that's all it is. I can probably live with poison-pen letters."

"You shouldn't have to."

"That's where you're wrong."

Matt instantly looked alert. "What do you mean?"

Here goes, Lord.

"The man who died?" Lorie swallowed hard. "I shot him."

Matt's defenses clanged into place. She'd shot and killed a man?

Judge not, lest ye be judged. The verse popped unbidden into his thoughts. Okay. There had to be extenuating circumstances. If he was patient, maybe she'd tell him.

He waited with the quiet expression that often got people to confess. Yet Lorie Narramore stood next to her desk, eyes filled with sadness, and said nothing else. Matt cleared his throat and, without stopping to reason why, pulled out one of his business cards and handed it to her just as Jen came to the door.

"In case you need anything else, my extension's on there."

"Thank you."

Her fingers brushed his as she accepted the card. A tingle shot up his arm. Never had Matt found keeping his professional calm such a struggle. Not good. Especially not with her confession still trembling on her lips.

"No tremble." *Oops.* "Uh, no trouble."

Matt fled. He made sure his steps were slow and steady, but in his heart, he knew the truth. It was flight.

He didn't feel secure again until he was safely in the patrol car.

* * *

"Well, that was certainly peculiar." Jen stood, arms akimbo, staring at the spot Deputy MacGregor had vacated.

"What?"

"Matt. I've never seen him so bowled over. I think he likes you."

Great. That was the *last* thing she needed. Lorie rearranged the neat piles of folders on her desk to avoid meeting Jen's eyes. "Don't be silly."

"I'm not. I'm being practical." Jen walked over and leaned on Lorie's desk, making herself impossible to ignore. "You're single. He's single. You're a Christian. He's—"

"Let it go, Jen. I'm not in the market for a man." *Especially not one in law enforcement.*

"But he's cute."

"So are puppies, but that doesn't mean I want another one." Giving the folders one last tweak, Lorie straightened up. "We have a library to take care of, or have you forgotten?"

Jen sighed, but gave in. "Okay. I'll make sure nobody makes off with the teen horror books."

"I'll be out in a minute."

Lorie waited until Jen was gone, and then searched the tiny room from one end to the other, looking under papers, under books, anywhere the note could have gone.

After fifteen fruitless minutes, Lorie tried to dismiss the note from her mind.

Getting some of the hobby wire she kept in her desk for the summer craft program, Lorie tied up the bathroom window the best she could. Winding the wire around the handle and the broken lock might not do much to keep anyone out, but it made her feel marginally better. Still, the door had also been unlocked. Had it been from the inside out, or was the window merely a distraction? However it had happened, the intruder also had gotten access to her locked office.

A shudder took her by surprise. She reached for the phone. Paging through the phone book, she found three listings for locksmiths, one of whom had married into her family.

Even if she had to pay for the installation herself, she was getting her office lock changed and the window repaired. Today.

Matt spent the rest of his patrol trying not to think about the new librarian. Filing his report from the car's computer, he entered "breaking and entering, intimidation, stalking" in the reason-for-call box. He longed to go back to the office and see what leads he could scare up, but that would have to wait until after his patrol.

To think someone might actually have it in for Lorie Narramore gave Matt a stomachache. She seemed sweet. Of course, you couldn't always tell by looking, but Matt believed she was what she seemed to be: a victim of circumstances forced into taking a life. It was obvious the experience still weighed on her, and he hated the thought that someone was deliberately making it worse.

Driving back on his normal patrol route through the lunch break traffic, he wondered where the new librarian went to church. Or whether she went to church. If she didn't, he had one more reason not to consider seeing her socially after this case was closed.

He knew from experience that a relationship where faith wasn't shared would only lead *him* astray. Back in high school, he'd been more optimistic. Lorene had been so vulnerable, so sweetly tempting that he'd ignored everything he'd ever been taught. She'd ended up breaking his heart, and he had no guarantee "Lorie" Loretta Narramore was any different from "Lorie" Lorene O'Hara.

Nope. He had to keep his head on straight and his heart

under control. There was no way he was allowing another attractive Lorie to get under his skin and wreck his good judgment. The first one had nearly ruined his life.

The radio crackled. "Unit 5, there's a fender bender on Highway 21. What's your location?"

Matt grabbed the mike and keyed it. "Dispatch, I'm eastbound on Hackberry approaching the intersection of Van Buren."

Another burst of static… "Paramedics are already at the scene, but we need you for crowd control."

"On my way."

Matt switched on the lights and siren and was at the scene in less than three minutes. Setting up orange traffic cones and diverting cars to an alternate route helped to get his mind off the librarian. He managed not to think of her for at least ten minutes, until the paramedic van took off for Lucius Dainger Memorial Hospital in nearby West Bluff.

As he put the stacked cones back into the trunk, another memory of Lorie Narramore drifted up from his memory. She'd been in the Diamondback Marching Band, playing the glockenspiel on the edge of the gridiron, when a tackle had tumbled him into the band. He'd ended up knocking her over and helping her up. Her glasses had rendered her light brown eyes enormous. Hmm. She wasn't wearing glasses these days, but her eyes were still amazing.

What was it about Lorie Narramore? He wasn't the kind of bachelor who was drawn to every attractive female in sight. Especially one who by her own admission had shot and killed a man. It wasn't damsel-in-distress syndrome, either. He had the impression she could handle herself in a tricky situation. So why exactly was he having trouble concentrating on work?

Maybe it was because someone had threatened the librarian. Once he ran the prints, maybe he could match them up with someone in AFIS and this case would be over.

Unfortunately, when he got back to the station, the prints

from the office were not in AFIS. Lorie's prints, however, brought up a large file.

Her mug shot looked strained rather than fearful or defiant. Huge purple shadows bordered her eyes. Her mouth was drawn.

The case had been through the San Diego County courts last year and had made quite a splash. Matt was surprised that it hadn't made the local news, but if it had, he'd missed it.

Grayson Carl, the man Lorie had shot, was a suspected drug lord, with ties to a network in Colombia and Panama. If she'd been sent to prison, the Orgulloso cartel would have had her assassinated before the year was out. Could they have been the ones behind the harassment in San Diego—and today's note?

Threatening notes and phone calls seemed a bit mild for them. Drive-by shootings were more their style.

The file was too long to absorb in one sitting. Matt sent it to the printer, including the court transcripts, to read at home.

"Working late, Mac?"

Matt looked up from his computer to see the sheriff's broad frame filling the doorway.

"A little. Getting some homework on that case your wife sent me on this morning." The laser printer spat out pages at breakneck speed. "What do you know about Lorie Narramore at the county library?"

Frank's sandy eyebrows rose. "I looked over your report. On the surface, the note doesn't sound like much, but, given her background, I don't like it. I was hoping she'd left her troubles in San Diego."

"Do you really see an international cartel coming after someone in our little county, Frank?"

"I wish I could say no and mean it." The sheriff ambled into Matt's tiny office and plunked down in the blue upholstered visitor's chair. "The way things have been going lately on the illegal-drug front, I'm not so sure."

Matt leaned on his desk. "I'm not going to find anything in here about Ms. Narramore that I won't like, will I?"

"Depends on what you don't like."

Matt wasn't happy with the answer, but knew Frank wouldn't say any more until Matt had had a chance to read through the file and come to his own conclusions. But what would he find? True, she'd been acquitted, but the nagging question remained.

If she'd truly been innocent, why had she ever been tried for murder?

THREE

Just as Lorie was about to depart for the day, her desk phone jangled.

"Leave it, why don't you?" Jen slung her purse over her shoulder and held out Lorie's. "You know it's past closing time."

"It might be Mom. Her church is getting ready for Vacation Bible School, and she has some idea I can help."

"Why wouldn't she call your cell phone?"

Lorie shrugged. "I'd better get it." She lifted the receiver. "Dainger County Library, Lorie Narramore speaking." Mom's cheery voice would pipe up any second.

A slight hissing was the only indication anyone was on the other end of the line.

"Hel-*lo,* Dainger County Library."

Lorie's repeated greeting brought no response. "Is anybody there?"

Jen made "hang it up" gestures with her free hand.

She'd give it five more seconds. "Five, four, thr—"

"Murderer."

Lorie froze. "What did—"

"Murrr-dererrrrr." The whisper was hoarse, drawn-out.

Not again!

Lorie slammed the receiver into the cradle. Her heart thundered against her ribs.

"What's wrong?"

Lorie shook her head, unable to speak.

Jen's eyes grew huge. "It wasn't Matt with bad news about the fingerprinting, was it?"

Lorie's mouth opened, but no words came out. Shaking her head, Lorie shivered.

"Okay, that settles it. You've coming home with me for supper."

"But—"

"No arguments." Jen shoved Lorie's purse at her until she took it. "It's just takeout from Old West Pizza, but you don't need to be alone."

The phone's ring shattered the stillness. They stared at it. Another two rings would take it to voice mail.

Jen's hand reached out before Lorie could stop her.

"Dainger County Library, this is Jen. How can I help you?"

A split second later she held out the receiver so Lorie could hear the dial tone.

Shuddering, Lorie clutched her purse to her chest. "You're right. I don't need to be alone."

Matt drove back to the Dainger County Library when his shift was over but one glance at the parking lot told him he'd already missed her. He'd forgotten; that was right. The library was open late only on Fridays.

He pulled the pickup into the empty parking lot and phoned J. T. Burkhalter. The voice of the family's four-year-old answered.

"Bookhawtew wesidence."

"Hi, Bobby. Put your daddy on, please."

"Okay. DAD-DEE! TEWEPHONE!"

Matt jerked the cell phone away from his ear at the first bellow, so he wasn't totally deafened when J.T. picked up.

"Hey J.T., it's Matt."

"What's up, bro?"

"Something strange happened at the library today. I wondered if Jen had mentioned it."

J.T. chuckled. "You mean the 'Puzzle of the Purloined Poison Pen?' She did bring up the subject a time or twelve."

"Could I swing by and ask her a few questions?"

"Sure. Come for supper. Jen brought home pizza."

Matt smiled. He hadn't been angling for an invitation, but pizza sounded good.

"I'll see you then."

Five minutes later, Jen opened the door when Matt arrived. "Come on in before it gets cold."

Matt keyed the automatic lock on his red F-150 Super-Crew and walked into the organized chaos that was the Burkhalter house. Bobby immediately tackle-hugged him around the knees.

"Unca Matt!"

"Hey, Uncle Matt's here!" Not to be left out, eight-year-old Kevin raced toward his honorary uncle, holding out his latest freebie from the fast-food kiddie meal.

"Ooh, scary dinosaur!"

His comment earned Matt an instant grin from Kevin, who growled and waved the green plastic tyrannosaurus in Matt's face.

Chrissy typed something on her phone, giggled and put it into her pocket before waving at Matt.

"New boyfriend?"

Chrissy shook her head. "Oh, no, Uncle Matt."

"Good. You're too young to date."

Chrissy giggled again. It was such a normal sound. How old was she now? Matt had lost track.

"I'm thir*teen*. All my friends are dating." Her phone buzzed again, and she snatched it out of her pocket to check the latest text.

"All the more reason." Matt thought of himself at thirteen, a mass of pimples and hormones. He shuddered. He was so thankful he didn't have kids. He wasn't sure he could take the stress.

"Jen, where do you keep the soda glasses?"

Matt started. Lorie Narramore was here? Alarm bells clanged in his brain. He whirled to face Jen.

"Upper cupboard over the counter next to the refrigerator." Jen rolled her eyes at Matt. "Turn off that expression, Deputy. I invited Lorie before J.T. asked you over, so you can stick your suspicion right back in your detective kit."

Lorie emerged from the kitchen carrying two glasses in each hand.

"Chrissy, put the phone away and help Lorie."

Chrissy barely missed colliding with Matt on her way to help. She snatched the glasses from Lorie just as Lorie spotted Matt. Good thing. It looked as though she'd have dropped them if Chrissy hadn't intervened.

"Deputy? Why are you—did Jen phone you?" Lorie still looked alarmed. Had the note been *that* disturbing?

Matt put a smile on his face.

"Nope. Just called to catch up with J.T., and he invited me for supper." Noticing that Lorie's expression hadn't changed, his trouble radar kicked in. "Why? Has something else happened?"

Before Lorie could answer, Jen called the rest of the family to the table. J.T. brought the two Old West Pizza family-size to-go boxes from the kitchen and set them in the middle as the thundering herd of children took their places.

"I want to sit by Miss Lowie!" Bobby announced.

In the table shuffling that followed, Matt ended up on Lorie's other side. J.T. held out his hands to Bobby and Kevin, who were seated next to him. The prayer circle quickly formed around the table. Lorie's hand was soft but firm. Matt wondered if she still played an instrument. He ignored the warmth that traveled up his arm at the contact.

"Lord, thank You for the guests You've brought us, and thank You for keeping us all safe today. Please bless this food and our fellowship, in Jesus's name. Amen."

A round of hearty "Amens" preceded an immediate scramble for pizza slices. Matt felt a gentle tug and realized he hadn't let go of Lorie's hand.

"Oh. Sorry." He released her.

"No problem." Lorie concentrated on the slice of pizza in front of her, effectively cutting off conversation.

The Burkhalter children chattered about upcoming church camp and dozens of other subjects. Matt could barely keep up. He did keep a surreptitious eye on Lorie, noticing as color slowly returned to her fine cheekbones.

Matt waited until after the kids had scarfed down their pizza and scattered to their rooms before bringing up Lorie's distress.

"Something else has happened since that note."

Lorie turned to look at him. She nodded slowly.

"What?"

"Somebody called." Jen spoke before Lorie could. "Just as we were leaving for the day."

"And…?"

Color drained from Lorie's face.

"She wouldn't tell me what he said." Jen sounded irked. "But it must have been pretty bad."

Matt waited until Lorie turned to him. Her anguished expression revealed more than words.

"You should have notified us immediately so we could put a trace on the call. Was it the person who sent the note?"

Lorie gulped. "I don't know. Maybe. Probably."

"So I insisted she come home with me." Jen took another swallow of sweet tea.

"Good idea." Was Lorie going to tell him voluntarily, or

would he have to drag the information out of her? "Well? What did he say?"

Tears formed in her eyes, making them glisten. She blinked them away.

"Just one word. It was enough."

Matt raised both eyebrows in a question.

Lorie took a deep breath, and, as she let it out slowly, breathed her answer. "Murderer."

Jen's hand flew to her mouth. "You didn't tell me! Oh, you poor thing! No wonder you were so shaken. Do you think *that's* what the note meant?" She reached over the table and patted Lorie's hand.

Lorie nodded.

"You were cleared completely." Matt's words were firm. "There's no reason you should have to put up with this kind of harassment."

Lorie flashed him a grateful smile.

Matt turned to look at Jen. "Speaking of the note, what was the story with the invoice you tried to hide from me?"

J.T. got the expression of a foxhound that had just picked up the scent. This was apparently news to him.

"It was for an order of books from a new publisher. One of the patrons put in a request. Unfortunately, he happens to be on the library committee in the county board of supervisors, so we had to order them."

What books would Jen find so objectionable? "Smut?"

"No." Jen sighed. "Worse. Books claiming the Holocaust never happened."

The pizza and salad soured in Matt's stomach. His grandfather had been among the troops that freed the prisoners at Dachau. He'd shown Matt the photographs, pictures of things he'd never imagined one human being could do to another. Then again, that had been the problem. The Nazis hadn't considered their victims to be real human beings. He fought against the rising indignation and managed to keep his voice calm.

"Who is it?"

"I don't know if I should—"

"Who?"

Jen sighed. "Supervisor Pitt."

Ouch. Joseph Pitt was a prosperous businessman who not only had friends in high places but was headed there himself. His radical beliefs hadn't kept him out of office. He always managed to gloss over the more controversial aspects of his beliefs when not among his fellow extremists. But, after a long conversation with the man at a social event when Pitt had been much the worse from whiskey, Matt knew way more than he ever wanted to about the repellant way the man's mind worked.

"Why didn't you tell me earlier?"

"I was embarrassed." Jen picked up her plate and headed toward the dishwasher with it, even though it still had leftover pizza on it. "I detest having that hate-filled propaganda in our little county library. But I need the job."

Matt looked at Lorie again. "Did you know about this?"

"Yes. When he explained why he wanted them, he said it was just to present both sides of the issue."

"And you believed him?"

Lorie straightened up. "Mr. Pitt has been nothing but good to me since I came back to Dainger County. He swayed the library board in my favor after they had second thoughts about hiring me. He even gave my Mustang a free tune-up at the Pitt Stop. I'm trying to give him the benefit of the doubt."

J.T. snorted. Matt flashed him a warning glance. Retreating behind his napkin, Jen's husband turned the snort into a cough.

"Supervisor Pitt has always been careful to stay on the right side of the law." Matt turned to Lorie again. "But I wouldn't get too close to him if I were you."

"Why not?"

Matt gave the obvious answer. "He's a politician. Isn't that reason enough?"

Lorie smiled, the first relaxed smile he'd seen since they'd parted earlier at the library. A surge of elation rose in him at the sight of it, and he squashed it. Lorie Narramore was a citizen, and he'd protect her as he'd protect any other citizen.

He had absolutely no reason to get carried away with emotion.

None.

Lorie was still sorting the books from the overnight drop when Jen arrived for work the next morning. She joined Lorie in the cubbyhole where they stored supplies.

"Any more notes?" Jen took a stack of books from Lorie and put them onto the rolling cart.

"No, thankfully. I'm beginning to hope it was just somebody's idea of a joke."

Jen snorted. "Pretty sick joke if you ask me. And what about that phone call?"

Lorie rubbed both hands up the sides of her face and through her hair, messing it up thoroughly. "I know. Yesterday seems like a bad dream." She scraped her hair back into a ponytail again.

"I hope you were careful driving home."

"Extra careful." She'd watched every driver with exaggerated caution, but there hadn't been any problems. Still, her dog and cats were nowhere close to being as happy as she was when she arrived home.

"Sleep okay?"

Lorie shook her head. "I kept hearing noises, but it was nothing, every time."

"Every time?" Jen's eyebrows rose. "How many times?"

"I don't know. Four or five." Lorie rubbed at her sleep-deprived eyes. "I'll be okay."

"I knew you should have stayed in our guest room. Then if you'd been woken up, you'd have known it was only one of my hooligans."

Lorie nodded. "I appreciate it, but in case things get ugly, I don't want your family in the middle of it."

Jen muttered something as she rolled the book rack out the door. It sounded like, "Things are already ugly."

Wednesday at the library lasted forever. A few regulars came looking for their favorite authors, but up till three o'clock, it stayed quiet. Lorie busied herself going through the stacks, checking to see whether any books needing repair had sneaked past returns.

As she was in the 799s, she noticed a book spine sticking out at a crooked angle. She reached up to shove it back into place.

Just as her fingertips touched the spine, she spotted a scrap of white sticking out of the top.

Fingerprints.

Lorie snatched her hand back. Could it be the vanished note from yesterday?

"Jen!"

"What do you need?" Jen appeared at the end of the row of shelving.

Lorie looked at her. "Do you see anything out of place?"

"No." Jen glanced around the stacks. "Wait, what's that?"

"I'm not sure. I think it might be the note. The book didn't look like that when I shelved it this morning."

A frown crossed Jen's face. "Was the paper sticking out when you found it?"

Lorie nodded. "I did touch the spine before I saw the paper, but I haven't moved it."

"Call Matt. Or Vangie."

Lorie reached into her pocket for her cell phone. "Could you get me my purse? I stuck Matt's card in there."

"Good choice." Jen grinned. "I'll be right back."

While she was away, Lorie looked at the book title. *Hunting and Gun Safety* by Oswald Smith. Her stomach twisted. Had the note been left in that book on purpose, or had it just been an unhappy coincidence?

Lorie fought against the rush of memory threatening to overwhelm her. *Not now, Lord, please.*

Jen returned with Lorie's brown leather purse slung over her arm. She tossed it, and Lorie caught it before it could smack her in the ribs.

"Thanks."

She found Matt's card in a side pocket and punched in the number with trembling fingers.

His phone rang once, twice—

"MacGregor."

"Matt, I mean, Deputy MacGregor, this is Lorie Narramore. I think I've found the note."

A jolt of electricity smacked Matt's middle when he heard the suppressed fear in Lorie's voice.

"Where?"

"Tucked into a library book that was put back crooked."

"Have you touched it?"

"I shelved it this morning—the note wasn't there then. When I spotted it just now, I only touched the spine, before I realized the note might be there. I hope I haven't messed up any fingerprints."

"I'll be there in about ten minutes. Don't let anyone else touch it."

"Thank you."

After reporting the call to dispatch, Matt drove toward the county library.

The parking lot was about a third full. Matt made a mental note of the vehicles. Three pickup trucks in various states of disrepair, plus one shiny new Dodge Ram belonging to the mayor's first cousin and a gunmetal-gray Mercedes-Benz.

Matt parked next to Lorie's car, a sporty blue Mustang convertible that looked as though it would be happier cruising down the Pacific Coast Highway than winding along the curves of Dainger County's hilly roads.

Matt locked his car door and headed inside. Jen stood behind the checkout desk, scanning a patron's mile-high stack of books.

"She's by the seven-ninety-nines," she said, before he even had a chance to ask.

"Thanks."

Lorie looked up as he rounded the stacks. Was that relief in her eyes?

"Thank you for coming."

Matt nodded then followed her glance to the book sticking out of the shelf.

"Is that the culprit?"

"Yes. Aside from the initial mistake, I haven't touched it. I have no idea whether that's the note, but it seems a little coincidental if it isn't."

Matt reached into his pocket for the fresh set of latex gloves. He slipped them on, pulling them in place with a snap.

Surprised by its weight, Matt nearly dropped the tome as he pulled it off the shelf. Recovering it like a fumbled football, he opened it to the sheet of paper. Crimson blood-dripping letters in font size 72 screamed at him from the page. He lifted his eyes to Lorie's.

"What was it the original note said?"

Lorie started. "Original note? You mean—" She took a deep breath. "It said, 'Don't think you can get away with it.'"

"That's what I thought. Can you explain this, then?" He held the page where she could read it.

Lorie went deathly white and staggered against the bookshelf.

BANG! HE'S DEAD, read the top of the note.

Halfway down the page, it continued: *YOU'RE NEXT.*

FOUR

No, Lord. This can't be happening.

Swallowing the bile that rose in her throat, Lorie struggled to find words. Matt would expect her to say something, not just stand there like a pillar of salt. First she had to keep from throwing up.

"Take a deep breath." Matt's voice penetrated the ringing in her ears.

Lorie tried, and had a fit of coughing. When she recovered, she took in as deep a breath as she could.

"Slowly. That's it. We don't want you to hyperventilate."

His right hand reached out to steady her, but pulled away almost instantly. That *zap* she'd felt at his touch must have been static electricity.

Please, Father. Please.

She couldn't even form a sensible prayer.

"You're not going to faint, are you?" Matt's voice was filled with concern.

"I don't think so."

Matt turned his head as a library patron turned the corner. Recognizing the man as Supervisor Pitt, Matt blinked. What were the odds of his showing up the day after he'd discussed the businessman-turned-politician with Lorie and the Burkhalters?

"Can you give us a moment, please?"

"Of course, Deputy." The stately, graying supervisor moved down the next aisle.

"Do you want to go sit down while I print this area?"

Lorie knew she was in shock. She needed a cup of over-sweetened hot tea. She put a hand to her face. Cold. So cold. Like that night—

No. She wouldn't let herself fall apart again. She needed to be stronger than that. It was the only way she'd get through this.

"Is it okay if I stay? I'll sit right over here on the step stool out of your way."

"Fine. Wait here while I get the incident kit."

Lorie nodded.

Matt left, carrying the book and that bloody-looking note with him.

Supervisor Pitt reemerged from around the corner. He gave her the same encouraging smile he'd had for her when he convinced the library board to hire her.

"Has the deputy finished investigating the shelves, Miss Narramore?"

"I'm sorry, sir. I think it's going to be a while."

Supervisor Pitt straightened his shoulders in a way that made him look much more vigorous than a man in his sixties ought to appear.

"I'm in a hurry, Miss Narramore."

Lorie knew exactly how Mr. Pitt felt. She was frustrated, herself.

"What book are you looking for?" The words came out of her mouth against her better judgment.

The look on his face went from impatience to satisfaction in an instant. *"The Art of the Decoy."*

"Do you know the call number?"

"745.4."

Lorie looked for the book, just down the aisle a bit from where she'd found the note.

Forget the note. Concentrate on the patron.

The trade paperback was stuck between two oversize hardbacks. Lorie worked it loose and handed it to Supervisor Pitt just as Matt came back.

"What are you doing?"

"My job. I didn't think you'd want anyone else in here until you'd—what do you call it—processed the scene."

"Exactly why I don't want anything to be moved." Matt held out his hand for the book.

Supervisor Pitt got a sour look on his face. "Young man, do you know who I am?"

"Yes, sir." Matt stood his ground. "Joseph Pitt, County Board of Supervisors, an *elected* official." The emphasis he put on "elected" was subtle, but it was enough to raise the man's blood pressure, if the rising color in his complexion were any gauge.

"Miss Narramore was simply handing me the book I want." He raised one impeccably groomed gray eyebrow. "If I am forced to stand around all day, I can't get back to my meetings and reports that allow me to allocate funds for this library *and* your salary."

"The library and I are both grateful for your support. We'll be even more grateful if you'll let us do our jobs. This is a crime scene."

"A crime scene? Here?" Pitt managed to infuse the maximum amount of incredulity and disdain into his tone. "Where's the body?"

In California. Lorie squeezed her eyes shut against the memory, but it didn't help. She could still see the man lying there, bleeding out, hear his last words, cursing her, cursing—

"Just because there's no body doesn't mean there hasn't been a crime."

Jolted back to the present, Lorie watched as Supervisor Pitt forked over the book, still looking as though his face could curdle milk. Strange. He'd always been so polite when speaking to her. After one last cold glare at

Matt, he left. They could hear his complaint to Jen as he stalked out of the library without checking out any books. Lorie ran both hands through her hair but stopped short of pulling it out.

"Of all the times for him to want to check out a book—"

"He's a blot on this county, even if he does own the best auto-body shop in the area."

Lorie blinked at Matt. He sounded so…angry. She knew he didn't like Supervisor Pitt, but his reaction seemed way out of line.

"A few more disgruntled patrons like the supervisor, and I won't even need my poison-pen pal."

"Let's deal with one thing at a time." Matt applied fingerprint dust to the area surrounding the book's place on the shelf.

Lorie covered her mouth and nose to avoid breathing the few particles that became airborne. It was like watching a crime show on television. She'd never liked them. Not after the arrest and— *Don't go there.*

Her thoughts turned back to the note, and its contents. Who here could know about California? Aside from Supervisor Pitt and the rest of the library board, her fellow librarians, her immediate family and closest friends…unless they'd told their friends…

Who could hate her so much? More importantly, how far were they willing to go?

Matt had an idea for the next step he should take—but he decided he'd better consult Frank first.

Frank answered the tap on his open door with a beckoning nod.

"What's the follow-up on the meth lab?"

Matt shook his head, frowning in frustration at the thought of the other case on his desk—the one that was going absolutely nowhere. "Gone. Nothing left but the smell in the air, a couple of empty propane bottles and a bunch of trash in the abandoned house. We did manage to lift some prints, but so far the computer hasn't been able to find a match. Probably amateurs."

"That's the problem with meth. It's too easy to cook." Frank closed a file on his desk. "And nothing to connect it to our old friend Leonard Adderson?"

"Nope." Frank and Matt agreed that the real-estate mogul was probably behind the meth labs popping up all through the county, but they hadn't been able to prove it. "Once again, it was on one of his rental properties, but we can't find evidence linking him to the actual operation. I keep hoping he'll slip up and be on-site when a call comes through." It was unlikely to happen. Adderson was as elusive as the snake his name resembled, and just as poisonous.

"So what do you need?"

"I want to ask Supervisor Pitt a few questions about the threats to Lorie Narramore."

Frank's fuzzy eyebrows shot toward the ceiling. "Your life insurance paid up?"

"I need to do this, Frank. There was another threatening note today—the kind of thing where you'd expect the perp to hang around and enjoy seeing the victim's reaction. Pitt was the only one around. What if he's the one behind the notes at the library?"

"And you're basing this suspicion on...?"

"Proximity. And he's run into some conflict with the librarians lately when he insisted that they order pro-Nazi literature. Maybe he doesn't like that they challenged his authority. Something to scare Lorie—Miss Narramore—might be his way of getting her back under his thumb."

"If he is responsible, we'll get him. In the meantime, you do your investigating quietly, from a distance. All right?"

"Yes, sir. And, sir…do you know Lorie Narramore's family?"

"I surely do. Her dad, Ben, and I play golf together and share a men's Bible study class at church. I don't really know Lorie, but I heard about the trouble she had out in California."

"She admitted to me she shot Carl."

Frank nodded. "When you read the file, you'll find all the extenuating circumstances that brought back the justifiable homicide ruling. I'm glad you're being thorough." After a moment's hesitation, Frank motioned for Matt to take a seat.

"You've already printed the note."

Matt nodded.

"Let's see it."

It was in the file he was carrying, so Matt passed the note, securely sealed in an evidence bag, to his boss.

"Plain and to the point. This is bound to be driving her nuts." Frank's expression was grave.

"She did seem frightened. I thought when I first showed it to her that she might faint, but she held up."

"If she's anything like her dad, she'll be made of strong stuff. Looks as if that's going to be needed." Frank stood. "Keep an eye on her, Matt. I have an uncomfortable feeling this may be just the beginning."

All Lorie wanted to do was forget the hateful note, but thoughts of it plagued her on the drive home from Daingerville. Before she hit the curves on Highway 21, she switched on the radio. Dainger County's own KDNJ sent a bouncy bluegrass tune into the updated classic Mustang. Lorie would have preferred silence, but her brain was too active for comfort.

After-work traffic made the drive home a challenge. The narrow two-lane highway was long overdue for major work, but Dainger County was low on the Arkansas Highway Department's upkeep list.

Thanks to all the traffic crowding her, Lorie was nearly to Buffalo Crossing before she noticed the car sticking close to her bumper. The heavily tinted windows of the Chevy Camaro looked out of place. She'd seen them often in San Diego, but seldom since returning to Arkansas. She tried to see if the black car had a front plate that might indicate if it were from out of state, but the driver stuck too close for that.

Tailgaters. It'd serve him right if I jammed on my brakes.

She'd never do that on purpose. She loved her car too much.

Maybe the driver just liked muscle cars, or was crowding in on her because he resented the traffic and poor road conditions slowing him down. Maybe. Or maybe not.

Lord, please, if he means any harm, stop him.

Heart racing, Lorie jabbed at the radio and shut it off. Light and shadow filtering through the branches made the road flicker like an old movie. Ordinarily, the wavering light didn't bother her, but her tailgater was making the drive extra nerve-wracking.

The Camaro edged closer as some of the traffic turned onto Highway 48 to Steeleytown. Lorie glanced in the rearview mirrors again. The car looked mean.

Don't let me panic. Lorie swallowed hard, fighting the rapid breathing that came with the adrenaline rush.

She couldn't let this clown follow her home. Not after the second note. Senses on high alert, billions of nerve-endings prickled her skin as the black car stuck to her bumper.

As she started down Rattlesnake Hill, the car edged over the double yellow line.

No, he can't pass me. Not here!

A booming blast from an approaching semi's air horn

forced the car behind her again. Lorie's heart raced. One more trick like that and he'd shove her off the hill.

Not taking any chances, hands clutching the wheel, Lorie concentrated on getting back onto mostly flat ground. If she could just make it to Cartwright, she could pull into the bank's parking lot and let this road hog have the whole highway. Unless he wasn't just a road hog…

Show me what to do, Lord.

Slowing as she wound around the hill bordering the eastern end of Cartwright Valley, Lorie drove into the small village, pleased to note that the car behind her eased off the gas, falling back.

Lorie turned into the bank's parking lot. As the car started to follow her, the town's lone black-and-white pulled to a stop at First Street. Lorie's heart pounded as the Camaro's driver headed on down the highway. She checked the license plate, but it was covered in an uncharacteristic amount of mud. No way to tell whether it was an Arkansas plate or not.

As the black-and-white settled in to watch for speeders, Lorie waited to let all the after-work traffic pass. After twenty cars and trucks had come down the hill, slowing noticeably as they spotted the police car, Lorie turned back into traffic.

Exhaustion tugged at her. She wasn't far from the turn-off to Wolf Hollow. Only a few more miles, and she'd be home.

For the rest of the drive, she scrutinized the traffic ahead of her, fearful of spotting her tailgater. When she reached AR Highway 14, she turned onto it without signaling. The small highway was practically empty.

She'd escaped.

Lorie slowly let out her breath. Most likely the driver had just been impatient, and glad to get out from behind her. That must be it. No connection between the tailgater and the missing library note.

If she could manage to convince herself of that, she'd sleep a lot better tonight.

After feeding her menagerie, Lorie debated whether or not she was too shaken to attend prayer meeting at Wolf Hollow Community Church. Everyone would understand if she didn't show up, knowing how exhausting her job could be. Still, she hated to miss it. Physically, she was well enough to attend, and spiritually, she needed all the help she could get.

Deciding she needed the fellowship more than rest, if she even *could* relax after being nearly run off the road, Lorie locked the dog and cats securely in the house and headed for the small town she called home.

Few people attended prayer meeting these days, but the ones who did were solid. Of the half dozen couples in attendance, one was her cousins the Tubbys, Tammy and her locksmith husband, Ike, whom Lorie hadn't been able to reach on the phone the previous day. Tammy pulled out a chair at the table in the fellowship hall. Lorie headed toward them, a human homing pigeon.

Tammy reached over and gave her a hug. "You look like you've been through the mill. Rough day at work?"

"Doesn't even begin to describe it." Lorie laid her worn Bible on the table and slung her purse onto the back of the chair. She launched into a brief description of the notes, the phone call, the broken window and the unlocked office door that they had firmly locked.

Ike frowned. "That doesn't sound good, but I can't say I'm surprised the locks didn't hold up. Those old locks should have been changed decades ago. Windows, too. A kid with a bobby pin could unlock them. You want me to come by tomorrow and have a look?"

"I was hoping you'd offer." Lorie leaned back in the

uncomfortable blue plastic chair as Pastor Enoch headed for the wireless microphone. Maybe she could relax, after all.

The next morning, Lorie arrived at work earlier than usual to meet her cousin-by-marriage. She showed him the damage outside then took him inside to the office.

Ike scrutinized the door handle. "It doesn't look like it was tampered with. Unlike the window, which I got to replace." His slow drawl sounded like home. The home where she'd forgotten she belonged.

"So how many keys are you gonna want for the office?"

"One."

"You should at least have two, so you'll have a spare. What if you lost it?"

"I'd call you."

Ike grinned. "The lock comes with two keys, anyway."

"Okay. I guess I can live with that."

"You know, if you really want security, you should get a different type of door. One without a window in it." Ike tapped the gold-painted OFFICE with a tan index finger. "Good blow with a hammer on this plain glass and they'd be right in there."

Lorie shrugged. "Technically it isn't my door. I'll have enough explaining to do to the county library board when they find out I authorized the changes."

Ike set his toolbox down onto the pinewood floor with a resounding clang. "You need somebody to back you up, just give us a call. Tammy and I'll speak up for you. Now, I'll get the measurements on the window after I fix the door. Should have it in for you by the end of the day."

"Thanks, Ike."

She left him to the work, the whir of his battery-powered drill driver reminding her of the leaf blower that used to stalk her neighborhood in San Diego. That noisy monstrosity was one thing she hadn't heard a lot of in Dainger County. She hoped that would never change.

The reminder of the place she used to call home turned her stomach to acid. Would she ever again be able to think of her dear city without raw memories of death's aftermath?

Only God knew.

FIVE

Jen arrived a few minutes later. Lorie met her at the door with the rolling book cart.

Tilting her head to one side, Jen scrutinized Lorie. "Something else happen?"

Lorie chuckled. "You should be a detective, not a librarian."

"Comes with the mom job description." She headed toward the office, but Lorie put out a hand and stopped her.

"Okay. Tell me."

"Somebody tried to run me off the road yesterday. I think."

"What!"

"I'm okay, car's okay, everything's okay. Not a scratch on either of us."

"But what happened?"

"It could've been just a tailgater with a death wish. He was way too close for miles, and then he tried to pass me on Rattlesnake Hill. A semi scared him back into his lane. I pulled off near a cop car and waited for him to go. End of story."

Jen let out a sigh. "I'm glad."

"Me, too." Lorie handed off the book cart to Jen.

"Okay, I'm on my way to the hardware store for that window. As for the door, you're all set." Ike moseyed back to the circulation desk, rusty red toolbox in one work-hardened hand, a set of keys in the other. He dropped them into Lorie's outstretched palm.

"Thanks, Ike."

"Tammy told me to tell you to come for supper Sunday night after church."

"Tell her thanks. I'll see y'all then." *Lord willing.* Odd how she'd gotten out of the habit of adding on the scriptural phrase while she was living in San Diego. "Lord willing."

Ike nodded, then headed out the door.

Moving the squeaky book cart toward the stacks, Jen stopped and looked back at Lorie. "What was that all about?"

"Ike just changed the lock on the office door. He'll be taking care of the window once he gets everything he needs."

Jen's jaw dropped. "When did you have time to get approval from the library board?"

"I didn't."

Her eyes widened further. "You did this on your own?"

"I won't charge them for it." Lorie fought the defensiveness rising inside her. Surely as head librarian, she was entitled to a few judgment calls.

"Those locks haven't been changed since 1958."

Lorie straightened her spine and placed both fists on her hips. "All the more reason. I had Ike put in a dead bolt."

"How'm I supposed to get in there?"

Lorie pulled one key off the tiny twist of wire and handed it to her. "Guard it with your life." She wiggled her eyebrows. "Seriously, just put it on your key ring and don't lose it. We only have the two. I guess we'll have to have another made for Mitzi's weekend shifts. Come on, let's check out the dead bolt and make certain both these keys work."

Lorie locked and unlocked the shiny brass lock with her key, and had Jen do the same.

The sight of the lock gave Lorie's spirit such a lift, she

broke into a grin. "That looks like it should keep out all but the most determined burglar."

Her good mood lasted only until closing. Lorie's heart began to race the moment she locked the door behind the last patron of the day. Soon she'd have to go home. Would the car that had almost driven her off the road be waiting for her again?

God has not given us a spirit of fear, but of power, and of love, and of a sound mind. Yep. That was true. But He also expected us to use the good sense He gave us.

Magnolia blossoms scented the summer air as Lorie and Jen reached the parking lot.

"See you tomorrow."

Lorie waved at Jen as she keyed the lock on her Mustang. It opened with a friendly chirp. Letting out a breath she hadn't realized she was holding, Lorie climbed into the car.

Lord, I can't keep reacting this way. Please help me.

Driving home, Lorie kept glancing in her rearview mirrors. She'd know that mean-looking car anywhere. If it followed her again—

It didn't. Her afternoon commute was completely uneventful.

Her dreams were another story.

Friday morning dawned with streaks of pink and purple daubing the horizon. Cardinals, white-throated sparrows and a persistent mourning dove greeted Lorie right after the three cats jumped on her bed and reminded her it was time for breakfast.

She blinked at them blearily. "All right. I'm up." Lorie shoved off her mamaw's multicolored story quilt and swung out of bed.

Colleen, the sable-and-white rough collie, wagged a bushy tail.

Mornings in Wolf Hollow were an entirely different

species from mornings in suburban San Diego. Here, no motorcycles vied to see which could be the loudest. That contest was reserved for the birds, whose chirping and calls made her glad she was here. Mostly.

After feeding the menagerie and herself breakfast, Lorie noticed the rural postal delivery pickup stop at her mailbox. Hannah was early today.

"Want to go to the mailbox?"

Colleen wagged and pranced by the door.

Throwing on a straw cowboy hat, Lorie opened the door for Colleen. The three cats raced outside, almost tripping her. Winken, Blinken and Nod had been impulse names that seemed to fit when she first met them, but proved to be appropriate only half the time. When they were awake, they were in constant motion. Off on a critter hunt now, no doubt. As long as they didn't bring home any rodents or birds, Lorie had no objections.

The morning air smelled of Old Blush China roses and magnolia blossoms. The tree-lined lane was alive with birdsong.

Then, suddenly, it wasn't.

Stopping in the middle of the lane, Colleen growled.

"What is it, girl?"

Nerves heightening, Lorie scanned the lane and the road for signs of intruders. Straining her ears to listen, Lorie could hear only the distant whine of a semi changing gears on Bobcat Hill.

No crashing in the underbrush. Only silence, with Colleen's low growl an undertone.

Lorie was halfway to the mailbox. Glancing back at the house, the sensation of being watched grew too strong to ignore.

"Colleen. Come."

Heading back toward the house, Lorie broke into a run. Something loud buzzed near her ear as her hat flew off her head. A split second later, she heard the report of a rifle.

Lord, help!

Lorie ran, Colleen keeping pace.

Another gunshot ripped through the meadow, a bullet thudding into the magnolia. Lorie ducked behind an oak. Why had she left her cell phone on the nightstand?

After darting from tree to tree, Lorie hesitated. There was little cover in front of the house. Could she make it inside without getting shot?

Wishing she had more experience with dodging and running, Lorie prayed and dashed for the front door. As she tripped on the step, a bullet struck the door frame where she should have been standing and ricocheted into the porch overhang. Lorie threw open the screen. Colleen bounded inside with Lorie on her heels.

Slamming the front door and locking it, Lorie raced to the phone and dialed 911. The emergency operator sounded rational and calm.

"I'm being shot at!" Tossing grammar to the wind, Lorie explained the situation in a few terse words.

"Can you see the shooter?"

"No. Please send someone soon."

"Relax, ma'am, and stay on the line. I've already notified the sheriff's department, and they have a deputy en route."

Lorie barely heard the reassurance, straining every part of her to listen for another shot. Colleen padded over to the window and looked out. Noticing, fear stole Lorie's breath for a moment, but she forced herself to speak.

"Colleen, come!"

The dog hurried to her side by the phone table and leaned into her.

The 911 operator was saying something else.

"What? I'm sorry."

"I asked if you have anyone with you."

Lorie reached down to pat Colleen's elegant head. "Just my dog. The cats are outside." The realization of their danger slammed a blow to her stomach. "Oh, no, my cats are outside." *Please, Lord, keep them safe.*

In the distance, the sound of a siren reached her ears. *Please protect the deputy, Lord.* The metallic slam of a door up on the road preceded a motor suddenly roaring to life.

"Tell the deputy I think the shooter is headed his way."

Matt was near the southern end of his regular patrol when the call came in from dispatch. The address on Wolf Hollow Trail didn't strike an immediate chord, but earlier in the month, he'd busted a marijuana growing operation south of there, in Oak Hill. Wondering if this call of shots fired was related, Matt turned left onto the Trail.

Moments later, Dispatch crackled over the radio again. "The shooter may be headed your way. Do you copy?"

Before Matt could reach for the mike, a black Camaro blew past him at three times the speed limit. Trying to turn on this narrow gravel-and-seal road halfway down a hill would be a nightmare. Frustrating gnawing at his stomach, Matt kept going till he came to the first driveway and did a quick three-point turn.

"Dispatch, this is Unit 5. I am in pursuit of a late-model, black Camaro, license unknown, heading eastbound on Wolf Hollow Trail. Suspect is presumed armed and dangerous."

Matt sent a prayer heavenward that whoever was driving the car *was* the assumed shooter. Otherwise, whoever had called in the incident was still in danger.

By the time Matt reached Highway 14, the car had disappeared. With hills in either direction, finding the driver was a fifty-fifty proposition.

"Dispatch, suspect vehicle is no longer in sight. What other units are in the vicinity?"

A burst of static answered him, followed almost immediately with words. "Unit 2 is southbound in your direction. Unit 15 is northbound." Another moment of silence, and then Dispatch came back on the line.

"Unit 15 has spotted the vehicle and is in pursuit southbound. Unit 5, see the woman. 153 Wolf Hollow Trail."

"Roger."

Matt switched off the mike and pounded the steering wheel. He'd come so close to apprehending the guy. Letting out a harsh breath, he reversed the car at the intersection and headed back toward the house in question.

Something about the address bugged him. It was on the edge of his brain. The knowledge eluded him as he drove slowly down the narrow country road.

Passing the mailbox with its numbers clearly attached to the side, Matt turned down the long gravel driveway and arrived at a once-white clapboard house that looked as if it needed more than just a coat of paint. A few of the shingles had blown off the roof. They appeared ancient, as if they'd been there since the higgledy-piggledy house was built. Massive oaks surrounded the place.

As he approached the house, the carport came into view. That blue Mustang looked familiar.

California plate.

It couldn't be. Could it?

What were the odds?

Parking the patrol unit, Matt got out and walked up onto the porch. He could hear a dog barking on the other side of the door. He was just raising his hand to knock on the screen door when the inner door opened.

The look of surprise on Lorie's face suggested she'd expected a different deputy.

"Matt." Her features relaxed, and she gave him a wary smile as she unlatched the old-fashioned wooden screen door.

"You're the one who reported shots being fired?"

"I was on my way to the mailbox, and I felt—I don't know, suddenly I thought I was being watched. When I turned to head back to the house, I heard a shot. My hat got knocked off."

"Show me where."

Lorie opened the screen door, its rusty springs squawking in protest.

A dog bounded out of the house ahead of Lorie. Making straight for Matt, the dog pranced around him as he held out his fist for her to sniff. A moment later, he petted her, ruffling the fur around her ears.

"Yeah, you're a good dog, aren't you?"

Lorie scanned the area, as if trying to sense whether the person who'd shot at her was still anywhere nearby.

A moment later, she apparently spotted the hat and ran to it.

"Wait! Don't touch it."

Lorie froze with her hand halfway to the ground.

No popgun had made that hole in the tall-crowned straw hat. Had the bullet struck just a few inches lower—Matt sent a silent prayer of thanks to the Lord that Lorie was still alive.

Lorie's case had just escalated from stalking to attempted murder.

Matt looked at Lorie as he pulled on latex gloves. "Please go back in the house and wait for me. I'll be in when I finish processing the scene." Lorie nodded and headed back to the house. As he watched her go, he noticed an additional shot that had bounced off the door frame. Right at Lorie's height.

After retrieving the digital camera from the unit, Matt began by photographing the bullet embedded in the porch overhang. He documented the entire area as he searched for the bullet that had struck Lorie's hat. When he found it lying next to the fence, twenty yards from the house, Matt whistled. The .338 caliber bullet had come from a long-range rifle. Whoever the shooter was, he or she meant business. It was only by God's grace that Lorie was still alive.

Matt picked up the bullet with latex-gloved hands. Sealing it into an evidence bag, he went to dig out the one that had struck the magnolia tree. Anger rose in his gut. He prayed he could catch this guy, before it was too late.

After he finished cataloging the evidence and stowing it in Unit 5, Matt tapped on the sagging wooden screen door. "Lorie?"

Lorie appeared with a glass of iced tea. "Perfect timing. It's sweet. I'm having to get back in the habit, after living so long in Southern California."

Matt accepted the tall glass, ignoring the sweat from the melting ice cubes. He took a long swig, swallowed and smiled. "You haven't lost your touch."

She held the door open for him, meaning he had to brush directly by her to reenter the living room. Even the fright she'd had couldn't overpower her sweet fragrance. Awareness twitched at him.

Get it under control, Matt. Losing your head again is the last thing you need—especially since you need your focus for the case.

Matt took another swallow of tea to clear his thoughts and refocus. He stared at the old upright piano, decked out in Victorian style, with an old-timey swivel seat set before it. So, he'd been right. She *did* still play an instrument.

Lorie waved a hand at an ancient horsehair sofa that might have been part of the original furnishings of the old house, if it hadn't actually been on the Ark, and seated herself on a fragile-looking rocking chair. Matt sat and immediately had to reach a hand to steady himself on the sofa's arm. Old as it was, the horsehair was still slippery.

"Sorry. I should have warned you about Dobbin."

Matt glanced a question at Lorie as he braced himself against sliding.

"It was my grandparents' wedding present from well-meaning relatives. Papaw named it for the song."

"Song?"

"One of their wedding songs had a line about hitching old Dobbin to the shay. Papaw said since he was sure they'd have a golden wedding day, it would be appropriate. I understand Mamaw tried to dissuade him, but once it took root with all their siblings and cousins, well…"

Matt chuckled. "Your grandfather sounds like he had a great sense of humor."

"He did." Lorie sniffed once and blinked rapidly. She tucked her feet up onto an ancient hassock that must once have been red and leaned back in the rickety rocking chair. "Much as I miss him, I'm glad he wasn't around for the trial."

Setting down the glass of tea, Matt leaned forward. "I've read the transcripts. I'm sorry it got so ugly."

"Thanks. God and my family got me through it, but it wasn't easy." Lorie ran a hand over her hair, ending the gesture by looking at her watch. "Oh, my, the time—I have to call Jen and get her to open without me, unless…?"

"I just have a few more questions. Call Jen. It shouldn't be long."

Lorie fetched her cell phone and completed the call with just a few short words, not explaining anything. Genuine admiration warmed Matt's chest. Not many people could manage to keep Jen Burkhalter to a one-minute call.

"Now." Lorie laid the phone on the coffee table. "You have more questions?"

Seeing her looking like this, so vulnerable and, aside from the dog, alone, Matt wished he didn't have to ask her anything about a case. Resigned, he pulled the notebook he still preferred to his smartphone out of his shirt pocket.

"Just a few. Particularly, one. Who wants you dead?"

SIX

Matt's question rocked Lorie.

"I've asked myself that repeatedly. According to everything the press could dig up, Carl had no family. His mother in Colombia was dead. The grandparents who raised him were murdered just outside Bogotá."

"Birth father?"

Lorie shrugged. "Who knows?"

"No siblings, cousins?"

Lorie shook her head. "He appeared to be the last of his line. As for his job, the hole in leadership must have filled immediately, though his death definitely slowed the flow of drugs for a long time. When I was in San Diego, I figured the harassment was because of the notoriety of the case. But here? I can't imagine."

"How did you first get involved with Grayson Carl?"

"Involved is the wrong word. We didn't move in the same circles at all. Before that night, I barely knew who he was. Afterward, most of what I learned came from the local news media. There was speculation, rumor, but never any real, hard evidence that he was the drug lord people suspected he might be. He had plenty of legitimate interests and was on a lot of charitable boards."

Lorie huddled deeper in her chair as her mind replayed the fateful night her life had changed forever.

"The library board decided to have a charity auction.

Since Carl was a well-known patron of the arts, they invited him to participate. That was their first mistake. Then they insisted all the senior librarians attend. Their second mistake. Why they thought big shots would want to hob-nob with the 'little' people beats me. Believe it or not, I thought my biggest problem was going to be what to wear." Lorie could hear the bitter tone in her voice, but she was beyond caring.

"We librarians had a table at the back of the room, not quite by the kitchen doors, but close. All the VIPs were nearer the front, including Grayson Carl. What nobody knew was that Candace Montoya, one of the county library board members, was apparently having an affair with Carl."

"Go on."

Lorie's stomach twisted and her heart began to race at the memories. "Near the end of the auction, Candace went to the ladies' room. I decided to freshen up at the same moment. Bad timing."

Lorie's head began to pound at what was coming next. She would have loved to banish the memory forever, but it always hovered just under the surface.

"Carl followed her into the bathroom lobby. From the raised voices I heard, it sounded like she'd uncovered his illegal activities and was threatening to expose him. All I wanted was to escape. I didn't mean to eavesdrop. When I finished drying my hands and entered the lobby, they were struggling over a gun. He made her drop it, and it slid straight to me."

Lorie shuddered. "When he saw the gun at my feet, he lunged at me. I tried to keep it away from him but we struggled over it. I can't remember exactly what happened, but the gun went off. The force knocked me to the floor. I can still hear his curses as he lay dying."

"Surely the local police assessed the situation."

"Yes. But Candace said the gun was Carl's. It turned out

to be unregistered, no telling where it came from. They tried to turn that against me at the trial. They also used the fact that Candace Montoya wasn't there to testify on my behalf."

"She wasn't?"

"No. After I saved her life, she ran away. She never showed up at the trial at all. The P.I. my lawyer hired tried to find her, but it was as if she'd vanished in a puff of smoke. She didn't even *try* to help me. I have such a hard time trying to forgive her for that."

"Anyone would."

"But how can I call myself a Christian and not forgive her? She must have been terrified the cartel would come after her." Another shiver racked her body. "I know I was."

Matt reached out and took her hands in his. Her hands were so cold. Warmth radiated into her.

"The police shouldn't have blamed you."

"Look at it from their point of view. The altercation took place in a bathroom, so there were no surveillance cameras to tell my side of the story. People embroidered freely, connecting me with Carl. Somehow, his people managed to plant evidence that he'd been sending me messages, to an email address I seldom used. I have no idea how they did that and managed to get the dates correct, but they did it."

"Hackers are good at what they do."

Lorie pulled her hands from Matt's warm ones and petted Colleen as if her life depended on it. "The trial was a circus. It's only God's grace I got off. Carl's people were outraged, and my life in San Diego County was basically over." A wave of nostalgia for all she'd lost washed over her.

"I moved as soon as I could get a buyer for my house. That took months. Sent off an application to the county board here, and since I got the job, I've been gradually fixing up my grandparents' old house. Now this. I don't want to have to move again. If it comes to a showdown…

This place has always been home. I don't know where else I could go."

Of course, that decision could be taken out of her hands at any moment.

"We're gonna get this guy, whoever he is," Matt promised.

Those wonderful blue eyes were so sincere. Lorie wished she could believe him, but, like the news media, the law had caused her nothing but trouble. She had no reason to believe this time was any different.

Back at the station, Matt carried the bullets he'd found to ballistics. Deputy DeShaun Bonney accepted the bag, grimacing at it.

"Hey, man. We got a backlog, you know?"

"I figured. But get to it as soon as you can, yeah? See if you can match it to any recent shootings, especially drug-cartel related. It's important."

Bonney raised a brunet eyebrow. "Cartel, huh? Your little meth-lab investigation getting interesting?"

"I wish!" Matt let out a sigh. "Probably not. It's another case. Put a rush on it if you can."

Heading to his desk to tackle the rest of his workload, Matt was disgruntled to realize he couldn't get Lorie the Librarian off his mind. Her story had been unsettling. From everything he could see concerning the confusing case, it was only answered prayer Lorie hadn't been convicted of premeditated murder.

Had the verdict made someone so angry that they'd flown here from California to inflict their own version of justice? Calls to the airports at Fort Smith, XNA, Little Rock and Tulsa had brought no satisfaction. All he'd gotten, besides the runaround, was a list of the airlines serving each airport. He typed up quick emails requesting passenger information for the past week to each airline, stating that he needed it for a case, and sent them off, feeling dissatisfied.

While still at his computer, Matt ran cross-checks on Lorie, doing searches on Google and Bing. On a whim, he visited her Facebook page. Not surprisingly, her privacy settings were high, and the only available information was her name.

While he was there, a streak of masochism had him key in his ex-fiancée Lorene's name. Her avatar showed her entire family: two sons, two daughters, and her husband—the man with whom she'd betrayed Matt, Owen Parkins. His former best friend. Her privacy settings were less stringent than Lorie Narramore's, and photos of their happy little family gnawed at Matt. Those should have been *his* kids, *his* photos. He glanced at her status.

"Thanks for praying."

Odd. Lorene had always ridiculed Matt's Christian upbringing. Why would she—

Not important. Matt closed the browser. He needed to concentrate on his case file.

Never had Lorie more looked forward to closing time. After asking Jen to take the weekend librarian, Mitzi, the key for tomorrow, Lorie locked up the library and went out to the almost empty parking lot. This was the longest Friday she'd had since the trial days.

When she got within keyless-entry range of her blue Mustang, she pushed the remote to unlock it.

The blast knocked her backward to the asphalt, sending white-hot flames into the night sky and dimming the streetlight.

Someone screamed her name.

Jen rushed over and reached a hand to her. "Are you all right? What happened?" She looked from Lorie to the flaming shards. Jen pulled Lorie to her feet.

"My poor car."

"Your poor car? What about *you?* Are you okay?"

"I—I think I scraped something when it exploded." Lorie swayed as a wave of dizziness engulfed her.

Jen held on to Lorie's arm and kept her from falling. "I need to call 911."

As Jen was reaching for her cell phone, they heard the first siren.

"Sounds like somebody beat me to it."

A fire truck rounded the corner, followed by a county EMS van. In a blur of motion, the firemen hooked up the hose to the fireplug on the corner and opened a stream of water strong enough to knock down a sumo wrestler.

EMS pulled into the parking lot and two techs in full gear ran over to Lorie and Jen.

"Who's hurt?"

Jen was quick to point them to Lorie.

"I don't think anything's broken." Lorie winced at the pain when one EMT took her arm gently. The two of them led Lorie to the van, with Jen trailing along behind.

The Mustang crackled and popped, the flames engulfing the chassis looking as though they never intended to stop burning. The firefighters kept the stream of water aimed at it. Lorie found it less excruciating to watch the car rather than the paramedics.

"No burns?" The man's voice was crisply professional, but still concerned.

"No, sir. Just scrapes and probably bruises."

The paramedic gently swabbed her scrapes with something that stung. "What happened?"

"All I did was activate the automatic lock. Then *ka-boom*."

The paramedic exchanged glances with his teammate. She could read the question in their faces. Car bomb?

Who would want to bomb her car? More than that, who had the resources to make it happen? This went beyond threatening notes, or even shots fired at her house.

Only one answer made sense: the Orgulloso cartel. And if a drug cartel was out to get her, then no place was safe.

Not here.

Not California.

Not anywhere.

Matt was still studying the pictures from Lorie's case file when Tiffany in dispatch rang his desk.

"Hey, you're working the librarian case, aren't you?"

"Yup. What's up?"

"We just took a 911 call from there. Fire department and paramedics have already been dispatched."

Visions of disaster sprang to mind. "What happened?"

"Car bomb, from the sound of it."

"Casualties?"

"Nobody dead, as far as they can tell, but one of the librarians is hurt."

"I'm on my way."

Three minutes later, Matt pulled his F-150 up on Choctaw Street next to the library parking lot. The sky was still ablaze, but it looked as though the fire department had a handle on it. Matt scanned the area until he spotted Lorie and Jen talking with a couple of EMTs. Lorie had bandages on both arms from just above the elbows almost to her wrists.

Matt struggled to keep his equilibrium as he made his way to the paramedic van. Was this morning's shooter responsible for this? If so, the stakes had escalated. Anyone could have been killed when the car bomb exploded. Things like this didn't happen in Dainger County.

Things like this didn't use *to happen in Dainger County.* Not until Lorie Narramore moved back from San Diego.

Lord, protect her. Keep her safe. And please let me solve this case soon.

Matt hurried toward the paramedic van. The sight of

Lorie sitting there, so pale, raised a flood of protectiveness normally reserved for his family members.

Matt squelched the impulse to hug Lorie, but he held out his right hand, and she put hers into it.

"You're certainly popular around here."

She gave him a game smile. "Yep. Life of the party. Came close to being the death of the party."

How could she joke about it? "God was looking out for you."

"For sure. If I hadn't gotten the battery replaced in my remote control…" Her voice trembled. "If I'd stuck the key in the lock…"

"You didn't." Jen gave her a sideways hug, probably to avoid hurting Lorie's arms. She looked at Matt. "What can we do to see about getting Lorie some departmental protection?"

Lorie shook her head. "Don't worry about me. I just… I'm more concerned about my family than I am about me. And Colleen and the cats, too."

Matt tapped her lightly on the shoulder. "What are your plans for tomorrow?"

"Calling my insurance company, for starters."

"And?"

Lorie's forehead creased, as if she were trying to remember. "Well, I had planned to go to West Bluff and do a little shopping, but that's off the menu now." She crossed her arms, winced and uncrossed them immediately. "Maybe see about getting a loaner car until I can get mine replaced. Although Mom and Dad would probably loan me their second car. I don't want them to, though. I wish I didn't even have to tell them about this."

Matt knew from skimming through the files that both her parents had flown to California to be with their only daughter while she was on trial. No way would they want her to go through this situation alone.

"You don't need to be out on that lonely place by yourself."

Fear flickered in Lorie's eyes. "I have to get back. Feed the dog and cats. Besides, it's home. Where else can I go?"

"How are you going to get home tonight?"

"I hadn't thought that far ahead."

"I can drive you out there and we can get your critters." Jen looked at her watch. "I think you should stay with J.T. and me tonight."

"No. I won't put you in danger."

"You shouldn't be alone." Matt hated the thought of her being isolated in the country, especially now that someone had blown up her car. He hadn't seen another vehicle on her property.

"I'll be all right."

"No. The situation is escalating way too fast. We need to discover who's behind these attacks, especially since you're now without transportation to even try to get away if someone comes after you. I don't want our next visit to be in the morgue." If she was going to be obstinate, he'd have to scare her into doing the right thing.

Lorie gulped.

"Matt's right. If you won't stay with us, what about your parents?"

"I can't take this danger to them any more than to you. I'll stay in a motel if I have to, but I don't want to put any of you at risk."

Jen shook her head.

"A motel won't let you bring your pets." Matt hoped he'd said the one thing that would get through to the stubborn little mule. "I'll run you out to your place, we can pick them up and then I'll take you someplace safe."

"Where?"

"My family's ranch."

"No way."

"Way or else." The words his nieces and nephews used so often popped out before he could stop them.

Jen nodded. "Great idea."

"No. Jen!" The tone in Lorie's voice was desperate.

"It's safe, and they have plenty of room, what with all the guesthouses. It couldn't be better."

"But I don't want—"

Matt interrupted. "I'll stay there, too, to keep an eye on things, so everyone will be under police protection. You won't be putting anyone in danger. You can call your parents from there, or we can stop by, if you prefer." He grinned. "And we take pets."

"I can't afford the Rob Roy Ranch."

"That's the beauty of it. As one of the owners, I can put you up for free."

Matt could see Lorie's hackles rise. "I don't take charity."

"This isn't charity. This is official protection."

"But—" Lorie winced as Jen backhanded her upper arm. "Ow!"

"Will you just take the man up on it?" Jen sounded irritated. She probably was. She should have been home at least ten minutes ago. Jen dug out her cell phone as the fire chief walked over from the smoldering hunk of melted metal and plastic that had once been Lorie's car.

"Fire's out, ma'am, but I have a few questions." He nodded at Matt. "Mac. Good to see you."

They bumped fists.

"Can it wait until morning, George? I think Ms. Narramore's about done in."

"I'd rather take care of it now, but I can see you're right. Let me know where I can find you, Ms. Narramore."

"Thank you." Relief colored her voice.

"She'll be at Rob Roy Ranch in one of the guesthouses."

Kershaw nodded. "I'll call you in the morning, then. You have a cell phone?"

Lorie rattled off the number, then reached out and touched the chief's arm to stop his departure. "What about my car?"

"Total loss, I'm afraid."

Tears welled up in Lorie's eyes. She must really have loved that car. Matt knew they'd made the trip all the way from San Diego together. In a few minutes it had gone from being a piece of home to a pile of smoldering rubble.

"I guess I'd better get my purse."

"You mean this?" Jen slipped Lorie's shoulder bag off and held it out to her. "I picked *it* up after I picked *you* up."

"Thanks." Lorie clutched the bag as if it were a life preserver. Matt noticed that Jen had clipped to the shoulder strap Lorie's now-useless car keys, which must have fallen from her hand in the explosion.

"Let's go round up your pets."

Lorie blinked at him for a moment. Being in shock, he expected it would take her a while to return to reality.

Taking a deep breath, she nodded.

"Keep her safe." With a couple of chirps, Jen opened her own car door. Nothing happened except the lights came on. "Guess my car's fine."

"I wonder how they knew to target mine...."

Matt placed a hand on her shoulder and steered her at a leisurely pace toward his SuperCrew F-150. "You still had California plates."

Lorie nodded.

"My insurance company isn't going to be happy."

"Don't worry about that tonight. You need to get somewhere safe so you can rest. You can think about things again tomorrow."

As she clicked the seat belt into place, she looked over at him, a wry expression on her face, visible from the cab's overhead light.

"You're right. But I still have to call my folks and let them know about this before they hear it on the news.

Not to mention…" Her voice trailed off as Matt started the engine.

She didn't tell him what she meant, but he could imagine. She was probably worried about her parents' reaction when they heard she was in protective custody on Rob Roy Ranch.

The dusk-to-dawn lights were shining when Matt drove Lorie up to her old farmhouse. The dog ran at his pickup, barking. Matt stopped the truck when it looked as though Colleen would throw herself under the wheels.

Matt got out, went around to Lorie's side of the pickup and opened the door. He held out a hand.

"You didn't have to do that."

"You're hurt, and besides, I'm a gentleman." He grinned. "I know that's a foreign term these days, but my family brought me up right. At the risk of being hit with handbags, I still open doors for ladies."

Lorie chuckled and accepted his hand. Once again, electricity coursed through his arm. Matt wondered whether she felt it, too.

Maybe she had. Her voice was a little breathless as she stepped down from the running board. "I won't be long."

"Let me go in first—I need to check the place out for you. Remember, they know where you live. Then I'll help you round up the animals."

Colleen pushed her nose into Lorie's hand. "Hey, girl." Lorie petted her and started when Colleen whimpered and backed out of reach. Lorie pulled her bloodied hand away in shock. She looked up at Matt. "She's hurt."

A premonition clutched at Matt. If Lorie's attacker had been to the house and hurt the dog, then more damage was likely. What would they be facing inside the house?

"Careful."

Lorie unlocked the front door and switched on the living room lights. Gasping for breath, she froze in the doorway.

The place had been wrecked.

"Stay back." Matt drew his sidearm and proceeded into the living room, picking his way through the broken bric-a-brac that littered the thin rugs covering the wide plank floor.

Behind him, Lorie was checking on the dog, making little crooning noises.

Aside from the contents being trashed, there didn't appear to be any serious structural damage. Matt switched on lights as he went from room to room, taking in the destruction.

Her bedroom was a large room on the east end of the house. In the middle of the bed, pinned to the shredded remains of a quilt with a long, thin knife, a note screamed:

EVERYTHING YOU HOLD DEAR IS FORFEIT.

Senses on alert, Matt felt rather than saw Lorie enter the room.

"No, stay back."

"I—oh. My quilt…" Her voice was mournful.

He glanced at her. The dog stood at her side, blood visible on the shaggy coat.

"They've done all this and all you can say is 'my quilt'?"

"Mamaw made it. For my tenth birthday." Her hand flew up to cover her mouth, as if she could hold back the sorrow.

"We've got to get you out of here and under protection immediately."

Lorie nodded. "If they've left me any clothes, I'll get packed."

The overturned walnut armoire held nothing but rags. The perp had even broken the heels off her shoes.

"Overkill." Matt's voice held contempt. "If they'd just wanted to make a point, they could have gone to a lot less trouble. They just did this to be cruel."

Lorie let out a sharp sigh. She sounded frustrated. "Well,

I obviously can't get anything else out of here. Everything seems to be badly damaged—including Colleen. I don't even know where the cats are. I'm afraid they're either hiding or dead.... Please, Lord, don't let them be dead."

Lorie's launch into prayer in the middle of speaking with him encouraged Matt.

Rubbing her eyes as though she could wipe out the desolation surrounding her, Lorie set her shoulders back. "We might as well go. Maybe you can stop by the Supercenter and let me pick up a couple of things for the night. Then we can drop Colleen off at the animal hospital."

"Let's look for your cats first."

She actually smiled at him, a real smile this time. With a hand on the dog's side, she walked through the rest of the old house, calling her cats' names as she picked her way through the debris.

The kitchen door stood open, the screen door unlatched. Lorie poked her head out the door and called, but the cats made no response.

"I think they must have escaped through the screen door when whoever did this showed up. At least I hope and pray so!"

Matt nodded, holstering his gun but remaining alert. When they'd locked the doors again, Matt phoned the situation in from the pickup. The night dispatch listened intently, and said to call back if there were any further developments.

Lorie fastened Colleen's collar through the seat belt in the truck's backseat before climbing in next to Matt. She seemed dazed and exhausted. Matt wanted to tell her everything would be all right...

But he couldn't lie to her like that. The creep who was after her was escalating his attacks. And things would get worse before they got better.

SEVEN

As they drove toward the outskirts of Daingerville, Lorie tried to focus on her surroundings, the vehicle lights zipping by, but her mind replayed everything that had happened over the past few days. Would the nightmare never end?

Matt stopped the car at the animal hospital. It was way after hours, but someone was usually there in case of emergency. As Lorie got Colleen out of the truck, Matt rang the after-hours bell.

"Come on, girl. I know it hurts."

Lorie felt like throttling whoever had injured her dog and scared off her cats, not to mention shooting at her, trashing her house and blowing up her car.

There's been enough violence and destruction. Lord, please, help me. I don't want to feel this way. The fear and unforgiveness are too much for me.

The door opened as Lorie led Colleen up the concrete walkway.

"You have an emergency?"

Lorie looked into the friendly face of a former classmate. Ginny Travis had always been an animal lover.

"Hi, Ginny. Mom told me you'd become a vet, but I didn't know you worked here."

Ginny smiled. "Yep, I'm Doc Travis these days. Good to

see you, Lorie." She brushed a strand of flyaway strawberry-blond hair out of her eyes. "What's the trouble?"

Matt spoke before Lorie could. "Somebody broke into Lorie's house and hurt the dog."

"Oh, no! Let's see." She looked down at Colleen, assessing her in the security lights. "This looks bad. What happened?"

"I'm not sure exactly. I think Colleen must have tried to stop the intruder."

Concern and warm competence glowed in Ginny's face. "Bring her on in to Exam Room 1. We'll be able to see better in there."

Daingerville Animal Hospital was bigger than Lorie remembered—though admittedly, she hadn't been there in years. Since the dog had already had all her shots when her parents presented Lorie with her, there'd been no occasion to visit the vet. She followed Ginny and Matt, bringing Colleen, who appeared to be upset by the various medicinal smells.

"It's okay, girl. I'll be right here with you."

Colleen whimpered as she accompanied them into the exam room. The three of them managed to get her up onto the table, which Ginny had draped with a large towel to keep the dog from getting cold.

Ginny got a good look at Lorie. "Looks like someone hurt you, too."

"Yeah, well, it hasn't been a banner day. How's Colleen?"

In the bright examining lights, Lorie could see where someone had hit Colleen with something sharp. It probably had been enough to send the dog running for cover.

"Well, the good news is that it doesn't seem life threatening. It doesn't look as if she'll need stitches, either. The bad news is, aside from the cut, she also has a lump. We'll clean the wound, put on some medicine which she won't like a bit, and then we'll bandage it. How does that sound?"

"Like a plan."

"You have vet insurance?"

"I wish."

Ginny chuckled. "That's what they all say. If you have animals, it's worth considering."

Lorie and Matt held Colleen still as Ginny went through the treatment. It wasn't as bad as Lorie had feared, but Colleen did squirm and protest. In addition to the bandage, Ginny put a cone collar around her neck to keep her from biting the bandage away.

Ginny checked Colleen's eyes and tested her reflexes, before nodding.

When it was done, they lifted Colleen down off the table.

"I don't think it's a serious injury, but keep an eye on her if you can over the weekend. If she starts showing signs of concussion—dizziness, upset stomach—either give me a call or bring her back in. And you should be able to take the collar off her in a few days. We'll make a follow-up appointment for next week to make sure she's healing properly."

"Okay."

"Let's run this through the computer, now that she's taken care of. I'll get the paperwork in order. I should have done that first, but I can't stand to make an animal wait while its people fill out forms. They don't understand."

Lorie smiled. "You always did care more about the animals than people."

"Some people, for sure."

Lorie filled out a new-patient form for Colleen, putting in all her contact information, most of which would be wrong for the next few days, until it was safe for her to go home again. If it ever was.

"At least the cell phone number is right. I'll be staying at Rob Roy Ranch until things settle down."

Ginny brightened at that news. "That's good. Colleen should be happy there."

"And safe." Matt's voice warmed Lorie like hot chocolate on a cold night.

"Let's set the appointment for next Friday at—two o'clock okay for you?"

Lorie nodded as she handed Ginny a credit card. After it cleared, they were ready to go.

Ginny gave Lorie a smile as she handed back the card. "Now that I know your number, let's get together for coffee."

"You may want to rethink that until after they catch whoever it is who's threatening me."

"We'll get together for coffee." No hint of compromise in her voice. Ginny reached out and petted Colleen. "After church Sunday morning good for you?"

Lorie smiled. "I may not be able to make it Sunday, but soon."

"Great! I'm so glad you're back in town."

"Thanks, Ginny. Me, too." *Despite everything.*

As Lorie fastened Colleen back into the truck seat, a sense of connection with Matt flowed through her. Maybe it was all the talk about church. Maybe it was relief that Colleen was going to be okay. For a brief moment, Lorie let herself relax, ignoring the intensifying pain in her arms.

They cruised through Daingerville, passing the collection of shops and buildings around the town square. At this hour, everything was closed and shuttered. The old gaslights glowed softly, illuminating their hanging baskets of multicolored petunias. Matt headed the pickup toward the Supercenter on the highway.

A few minutes later, Matt pulled into the parking lot and circled slowly, looking for a place.

"I'll come in with you."

Lorie shook her head. "I won't be long. Somebody needs to stay with Colleen."

In the glare of the overhead lights, Matt's eyes were warm and concerned. "I don't feel right about your going in alone."

"Then take me on to the ranch. I'll get what I need in the morning."

"You'll need some basic stuff tonight."

Since she hadn't found a single undamaged piece of clothing in the house, Lorie knew Matt was right. The ranch guesthouse probably had amenities like toothpaste and shampoo, but not nightclothes or slippers. What to wear to work on Monday loomed large in her thoughts. Lorie didn't ordinarily buy work clothes at the Supercenter, but she could make an exception for now.

"Let me go in by myself. I'll be fine. They have all those cameras. If anybody tries to bother me, I'll call for help."

Matt slid the car into a parking spot and turned off the engine.

"Hand me your cell phone."

Puzzled, Lorie handed it over. Matt punched a few buttons. A moment later, apparently satisfied, he handed it back.

"You didn't have anything special on speed-dial 9. Now you do. If you need me, call 9. I'll be right in."

A little glow of warmth touched Lorie's heart. She hadn't expected Matt to go that extra mile. Of course, maybe he was just doing his job, preventing her from being attacked. Maybe it was only a little deputy work. Sure. That must be it.

"Thanks." Lorie stuffed the phone into her pocket and activated the Bluetooth device at her ear. "It shouldn't take long. Maybe twenty minutes. Ten if I hurry and don't get stuck in a long line. Oh, should I get a few groceries while I'm here?"

"See, that's why I should come with you. I could point out the things you won't find at the ranch."

"Honestly, I'll feel much better with you keeping an

eye on Colleen." Lorie peered over the backseat. Colleen stretched and lay down, sighing.

"Hurry back."

Lorie nodded. She had no intention of dawdling.

Once inside the store, Lorie grabbed a bag of Colleen's favorite dog food, then headed for the women's department.

As she moved through the selection of Misses sizes looking for a shirt and skirt, the hair on the back of her neck stood up. Recognizing the sensation for the warning it was, Lorie stopped to look around. Someone was watching her.

After one complete circle, Lorie hadn't spotted anyone staring in her direction, and started to feel grateful that her initial panic hadn't made her phone Matt. Would he have come charging in here, gun drawn, scaring everybody?

Glancing up, she noticed one of the smoked-glass camera globes. Well, *naturally* she was being watched. Everyone was.

Not that there were too many people here on a Friday night after 10:00 p.m. Lorie shook off the spooky feeling and chose a couple of shirts in her size without trying them on. She might not feel like shopping tomorrow after everything that had happened today.

Picking out a skirt and a pair of jeans, nightclothes and underwear, Lorie moved to the limited selection of dressier items. She found something immediately. She wondered what Mom would say if she showed up at First Church in a dress from the Supercenter. In spite of everything, she smiled at the thought. First had a reputation for stuffiness.

Her own church wouldn't mind. Wolf Hollow Community was a little church, and, being out in the country, people often showed up in work clothes. Of course, she might not be going to her own church on Sunday. Matt might insist she accompany him to his. A little trickle of warmth settled in her interior at the thought.

Lorie shook herself, went to the shoe department and grabbed house slippers, shower shoes and a pair of dressy gold sandals for Sunday, in case she couldn't shop tomorrow.

Lorie's cell phone started playing Mozart in her ear, and she jumped.

Lord, I'm nervous as a feral cat. Please keep me safe.

She pressed the button on her Bluetooth earpiece. "Hello?"

"Are you all right? It's been twenty minutes."

Matt. Lorie sighed with relief.

"Yes. I'm sorry. It's taking longer than I thought."

"Did you remember your vitamins, makeup, little stuff like that?"

"No. I was concentrating on the big stuff." The memory of seeing her makeup, toothpaste and toiletries smeared all over her bathroom, not to mention the stench of three combined perfumes overpowering the spilled shampoo, washed over her again.

Some unknown enemy had gone into her house and deliberately ruined all of her things. Someone had left three threatening notes. An enemy had shot at her, blown up her car. Someone who hated her had injured Colleen.

Apparently the silence on her end made Matt nervous.

"Do you need me?"

Yes. But she didn't want to need him. Didn't want to have to need anyone in order to feel safe.

"How's Colleen?"

"Sleeping soundly. She'll be fine if I leave her."

Lorie hesitated only for a moment. The sense of being watched was too strong to ignore, security cameras or no security cameras.

"Okay. I'll meet you by the vitamins."

"Be right there."

A couple of chirps from her earpiece let her know he'd disconnected. As Lorie aimed her basket toward the front of the store, the sensation of being under observation heightened. All the fine hair on the back of her neck rose to attention.

Rules from the self-defense courses she'd taken in California echoed in her brain. *Always walk purposefully, as though you have a definite goal and destination in mind. Look confident. Criminals would rather attack people who appear weak or frightened.*

Straightening her spine, Lorie strode toward the pharmacy. If someone was going to bother her, she refused to be an easy target.

At this hour, most of the people she saw in the store were employees, though a few tired parents pushed carts with cranky babies on board. Nobody seemed to be at all interested in her. Still, if it wouldn't have looked weird to run, Lorie would have flown down the aisles to the pharmacy.

Matt looked up from the multivitamin shelf as Lorie raced toward him with a shopping cart. She had to be breaking the speed limit. Fortunately, no one was in her way.

"In a hurry?"

Lorie screeched to a halt two seconds before the cart would have hit him.

"Um. No. Not really."

Matt gave her a look. "What's really going on?"

"Nothing. I mean, it felt like someone was watching me, but I didn't see anybody."

Matt gave the aisles behind Lorie a quick once-over. No one there. His senses jumped to high alert.

No one had asked Matt to look after Lorie, officially, but it was something he'd had to do. The Lord had nudged him as surely as if He'd been standing at his shoulder when Matt made the offer of a cabin at the guest ranch.

"The sooner we get out of here, the better."

"You're not laughing at me?" Her voice sounded relieved.

"No. I'm not humoring you, either. Grab some vitamins and a toothbrush, and we'll get out of here."

"But—"

"No buts. Groceries can wait. We always have plenty of food in the ranch kitchen."

Lorie nodded.

The young cashier at the nearest checkout counter looked tired, the purple spikes of his hair matching the shadows under his eyes.

"Find everything you needed?"

"Yes, thanks."

Lorie ran everything through the checkout without speaking. Maybe she was more spooked than he'd thought. Given the day she'd put in, he could understand.

It was a relief to walk outside into the velvety night.

Matt was on high alert as he helped Lorie carry the bags out to the truck, but couldn't spot anything out of the ordinary. If someone had been following her, his presence must have frightened them off.

They locked the packages into the aluminum toolbox in the truck bed. By the time they got into the front seat, Colleen was awake. Her tail thumped against the gray leather seat.

"That's right, girl…we're back."

As they turned out onto Highway 273, Lorie sighed.

"All right?"

"Yes." Lorie sounded tired. "Thanks for making me do this."

"Anytime."

"I'm not usually so…"

Matt waited for her to continue, but she left the sentence hanging. "So…?"

"I'm not usually such a fraidy cat."

"You don't usually get shot at or your car blown up, either, I'm guessing."

Lorie chuckled. "True. I just wanted you to know."

"You have an even bigger ordeal ahead of you tonight."

She looked over at him sharply.

"What could be worse than flying bullets, exploding cars, my house being trashed and my dog being hurt?"

Matt grinned. "Officially meeting my family for the first time."

EIGHT

Lorie hadn't thought it was possible to feel any more trepidation than she had when she'd walked through the door of her house to find it in shambles. Matt's comment changed everything. By the time they pulled up to the gates at the Rob Roy Ranch, her stomach could have used a gallon or so of antacid.

She knew *about* Matt's family, of course. While not on quite the same social footing as the Daingers, the Holts, or the Steeleys, they still carried a lot of weight, especially in the farming and ranching community. Under normal circumstances, she'd have been happy for the chance to meet them.

These weren't exactly normal circumstances.

What bothered her the most, though, wasn't the idea of an awkward introduction, but rather the reason behind it. She hoped his siblings wouldn't be put in too much danger from their unexpected guest.

Matt drove up in front of the lodge and parked. "Wait here. I'll go grab the keys for you."

Lorie nodded. She was too exhausted to argue.

As she sat, waiting for Matt to return, Lorie's stomach started to growl. She had been too keyed up to feel hungry, but the adrenaline was wearing off. She'd bought food for Colleen but nothing for herself, not even an energy bar. Stupid.

No. Not stupid. Just the shock.

Lord, thank You for taking care of me. Thank You for letting Colleen be okay. Please protect Winken, Blinken and Nod.

The door to the lodge opened and Matt emerged, followed by another man who looked about the same age, not that it was easy to tell in the moonlight. Both men carried packages of what she hoped were food. Light glinted on aluminum cans.

Matt opened Lorie's door and handed her a zipper bag with bread in it and two cans of cola. "Meet my brother Jim. He runs the ranch."

"A pleasure," Jim said with a friendly smile.

"You, too." When had she fallen into the simple California responses? About the third year she'd lived there? Lorie wished she still sounded as though she belonged in Dainger County.

Jim handed her a covered glass dish, a bag of salad and a bottle of dressing. "Hope you like barbecue, 'cause that's what was already fixed. There's a microwave in the cabin. Matt'll show you how to work it."

Lorie's chest grew tight. She fought back more tears and managed to whisper thanks. Jim closed her door and Matt climbed into the pickup.

He clicked his seat belt, glanced over at her then started the engine. "Glad you still have your seat belt on."

"It's a habit."

"A good one. You do know it's the law in Arkansas now?"

Lorie chuckled. "Considering the hour I spent trying to calm Mom down once it passed, yes, I'd say so. I had to send her one of those emergency seat belt cutter/window-smasher combos before she was convinced she wouldn't be trapped inside a burning car."

"I keep one in every vehicle. You never know."

The image of her beautiful Mustang exploding made

Lorie swallow hard. If she'd gotten into her car and turned the ignition tonight… A shudder rumbled through her.

Matt drove up slowly beside an empty cabin and parked. A front-porch light glowed invitingly, as did the lights on all the cabins, occupied or not.

"Let me get that stuff before you try to get out." Matt came around and unloaded her lap.

"I can take some of it."

When Matt smiled, Lorie's stomach danced. Oh, dear. This was so bad. She could think of a million reasons why it wasn't a good idea to be attracted to Matt. Well, maybe not a million. But close.

Matt unlocked the door, and, after he switched on the light, Lorie followed him into a small living/dining/kitchen combination. A native stone fireplace graced one corner. An open Western-style armoire held a big-screen TV, stereo and combination video player.

Lorie had never been to the ranch, but she'd visited their website, so the Wild West–style furniture didn't surprise her. Its red-and-black buffalo plaid would be equally at home in Montana.

Ancient Rob Roy Tartan, her brain whispered.

"Come on in. The microwave's over here."

The microwave nestled close to an almost regular-size refrigerator, a sink, a tiny dishwasher and a coffeemaker.

Matt put the covered dish into the microwave, removed the plastic lid, stuck a paper towel over the top and set it for a couple of minutes to warm. "Dishes are in the cupboards, and glasses. They're clean. We run everything through the main dishwasher when guests leave."

"That's good." Lorie remembered something. "I forgot to buy a dog dish for Colleen."

Matt reached under the sink and pulled out a twin food/water dish. He ran tap water in the half labeled Water.

"I told you, we take pets. Some people always forget to bring the basic necessities for their animals. And given your situation, it's really not surprising that something slipped your mind. You're doing well to be functioning at all after the day you've put in."

Matt set the dish on the floor. Lorie tried not to notice the way his muscles flexed against his uniform, but failed. He just looked too good.

Lord, please help me. I don't want to be attracted to a deputy sheriff. The sensation of being iron filings to his magnet refused to dissipate.

While the barbecue warmed, they brought in Colleen and the purchases. Lorie carried the bags of clothes and toiletries into the bedroom. Wild horses raced across a fantasy desert landscape on the printed bedspread, but they barely registered.

Please, Lord. You know how I feel about lawmen.

Hearing the microwave beep, she laid her purchases on the bed and went back into the other room.

Matt had already poured Colleen some kibble and was putting salad into bowls when Lorie returned.

"You didn't have to do that."

He looked over his shoulder at the sound of her voice. "I don't mind," he said with a smile. "I hope you don't mind my eating with you."

"Not a bit." *Although that does make this seem awfully much like a date. Which it isn't. It's police protection. Not a date. Yeah, keep reminding yourself.*

Matt shoveled barbecue onto thick slices of home-baked bread. It smelled ambrosial. A memory of San Diego County's best barbecue places surfaced. Good 'cue was expensive out there. If the Ranch offered this on the menu, it was probably expensive here, too.

Matt poured the cola into glasses and set them on the table as Lorie sank into a chair. He sat across from her at the round oak table and held out his hand. He wanted to hold her hand?

* * *

Lorie looked surprised when Matt held out his hand to her. Didn't she pray before meals? She had at the Burkhalters'.

"Let's say grace."

The puzzlement cleared from her brow, and she put her hand into his. Matt immediately realized the action was a mistake. Warmth flowed from her fingers straight to his heart.

Please, Lord, help me stay focused on why she's here.

"Lord, we thank You that Lorie wasn't seriously hurt this day. We ask You to continue to keep her safe in Your loving care. Please bless this food to the good of our bodies, and keep our hearts and minds stayed on You, our perfect peace. Amen."

"Amen."

Matt looked into Lorie's eyes. Tears filling them made her eyes look like autumn leaves lining a creek bed. Mesmerized, Matt couldn't look away. After a moment, Lorie tugged at her hand. He hadn't realized he still held it. That was getting to be a habit.

"Oh. Sorry."

Lorie shrugged. "Not a problem, except that I'm hungry." She picked up half of the sandwich Matt had cut for her and bit into it. An expression of pure delight crossed her face as she chewed.

"Henny does make great barbecue, doesn't she?"

Lorie nodded, unable to speak with her mouth still full.

"She makes a good breakfast, too, but I want you to sleep in tomorrow if you can."

Lorie swallowed. "I'm used to getting up early, even on Saturday."

"It's late now and the cola's decaffeinated. If you're able to get some solid sleep, don't worry that you'll have to turn up early for breakfast. Henny will make you something no matter what time you need it."

"Are you sure it's a good idea for people to know I'm here?"

Matt pondered that a moment. "You're right. Call me when you wake up in the morning, and I'll bring something over."

"I don't want to put you to any more trouble."

"Get this straight, Lorie." He leaned over the table and made certain she was paying attention. "When somebody tries to blow up someone on my watch, I take it personally. So don't get upset with me if I seem a little overprotective."

"I'm just a case, Matt." Her voice was soft and held— what? Regret?

"Maybe in the beginning." He hadn't meant to verbalize the thought, but it was true. Sometime between the first call about the note and finding her house trashed, Lorie had become much more than just a case to him.

A flash of awareness in her eyes told him he wasn't the only one feeling the attraction. This situation had the potential to go either way.

Pull back. Things are complicated enough with her already. You can't afford to get involved emotionally.

Unfortunately, that ship had not only left the harbor, it was way over the horizon.

The air was thick with emotion. Lorie wasn't quite certain what to do about it. The situation she was in was psychologically draining enough all on its own—she didn't need the complication of a new relationship on top of it. And even if she was looking for someone, she'd never expect to find him in the sheriff's department. But she couldn't deny the way that Matt made her feel.

Just when the butterflies were threatening to break free of her innards and fill the room, Colleen came and put her head in Lorie's lap, cone collar and all. The sigh that escaped her doggie lips fluttered the paper napkins on the table.

"It does smell good, doesn't it, girl? And it is, but I don't think you should have any."

Colleen whined.

"She's smart." Matt's voice was admiring.

Lorie nodded. "Too smart for her own good, sometimes."

"The barbecue won't hurt her, unless she's sensitive to tomatoes."

"I can give her some leftovers, then?"

"Yup. Although not if you're trying to keep her from being spoiled."

"It's a little late for that, I'm afraid." Lorie slipped a bite of meat to Colleen, who took it daintily as her tail thumped the floor.

"Good dog."

"She is. It makes me sick that someone hurt her."

"You heard Doc Travis. She'll be fine."

"But still…"

"I know. When I find the person responsible for all this, I'm tacking on an animal-cruelty charge with the rest of it."

Lorie smiled. "That ought to be good for a year or two, right?"

"Right. People take animals seriously here in Arkansas, in case you don't remember."

"I remember."

Matt leaned forward. "And I take the safety of you and yours very seriously. You believe that, don't you?"

"I do," she said, meaning every word. She might not be ready for any kind of relationship with Matt MacGregor, but she knew she could trust him—knew she'd be safe tonight, under his protection.

For now, that would have to be enough.

NINE

"I'm okay, Mom, really. Just a little bruised and scraped up, but nothing serious." And exhausted from a terrible night's sleep...but there was no reason to mention that.

"You should have called the minute this happened! And why aren't you here?"

The question Lorie had dreaded. "I wasn't going to put you and Dad in danger."

"Well, you'd better come today." Mom sounded fearful. "Your dad and I can protect you."

"I'm fine here at Rob Roy Ranch. I know you must be worried—"

"Worried doesn't begin to describe it! When I think you could have been killed—"

"The Lord took care of me, Mom. And that's not going to change." Peace filled Lorie's heart when she spoke the words. Affirmation. God *was* taking care of her, no matter what happened.

"What about work?"

"I don't have to go in till Monday. Right now, I'm starving. I haven't had breakfast yet."

"I feel so bad, your staying way out there at the ranch."

"I'm in protective custody."

Mom sighed. "I know what *that* means. You're stuck. Can you at least come here to church tomorrow?"

"I don't know. I guess I'll go wherever Matt takes me, if he lets me off the ranch."

"Well, if he doesn't, at least you can get Pastor Burnett on TV."

The conversation turned to more comforting things, and ten minutes later, Lorie managed to hang up and call Matt.

"Ah, you're finally awake." Matt sounded relieved. "When did you get to sleep?"

"About four-thirty."

"You haven't slept long enough."

"I've slept as long as I can. I'm starving. You said something about breakfast."

"What'll you have?"

"Anything, and a lot of it."

"I'll be there in about ten minutes."

Matt disconnected, leaving Lorie feeling oddly disoriented. Being snatched out of her comfortable routine did that to her. She hated change. She'd thought she'd live in her sweet little house in Scripps Ranch until she married, or even afterward. Moving had nearly destroyed her.

Now here she was again, having to adjust to more change.

Colleen padded over to the door and whined.

"You need out, girl?"

Colleen answered with a sharp bark.

Lorie realized she hadn't brought Colleen's leash. It was a wonder she'd even remembered to bring the dog, considering the state of last night's agitation.

"You'll have to wait a minute while I come with you. That means I need to get dressed." *Oh, and Matt will be here any minute, too. I don't want him to catch me looking like this.*

The wood-framed bathroom mirror told her she didn't look as bad as she'd expected. Pale, yes. Untidy, yes, but not irreparably so. She shrugged into the jeans and a teal T-shirt she'd bought yesterday, and slipped into her work shoes that she'd worn the previous day, wishing she'd seen a good pair of sneakers at the store. Still, the comfy beige flats would be better than the sandals she'd bought to wear to church.

As she was about to open the door to let Colleen out, Matt knocked.

"Room service!"

Lorie opened the door and did a double take. Matt held a large walnut butler tray loaded down with covered dishes, a small pot of coffee and a Southwestern vase containing a cheery white African daisy.

"That looks wonderful." She took an appreciative sniff of the mingled aromas of bacon and eggs, fresh toast and strawberry jam rising from the tray. "And smells delicious."

Her stomach growled and Lorie felt the beginnings of a blush. "I've got to let Colleen out."

Matt set the tray down on the table. "Why don't I take her for a walk while you get some food in you?"

"Aren't you going to join me?"

"I ate breakfast three hours ago. I'm almost ready for lunch. I brought enough coffee for two, though, unless you're really thirsty. I'll join you in a few minutes."

If this was protective custody, it was beyond the call of duty. "Okay. Thanks."

Matt had brought a leash with him, tucked into his pocket. Now he snapped the end of it onto Colleen's collar, wiggled his eyebrows and shut the door after them.

I could get used to this, Lord.

A fragment of scripture floated into her brain. "Exceeding abundantly above."

Lorie prayed quickly over the food and dug in.

Matt paused beside a pecan tree where Colleen was occupied. "I thought your owner would never wake up."

Colleen woofed gently.

Matt chuckled. "I see you agree with me. But she's awake now."

Colleen wagged her tail, and then pulled on the leash, straining to get back to the cabin, despite the scolding attention of squirrels in a nearby oak.

By the time Matt and Colleen got back, Lorie had decimated breakfast.

"You really were hungry, weren't you?"

Lorie blushed, as if embarrassed to have a healthy appetite. "Apparently almost being blown up will do that for a girl."

Matt laughed. "At least you haven't lost your sense of humor."

"I consider humor a gift from God to help us through rough times."

Colleen pulled against the leash as Matt let her loose. "Yours must have been strained to the limit the last couple of days."

"Not as much as during the trial, but, yeah. It's been a challenge. Listen, I called my mom this morning, and she was seriously upset I hadn't let her know what happened last night."

"Understandable."

"I think she really wants to see me in person, just so she can see for herself that I wasn't badly hurt. She asked if I could go to First with her and Dad tomorrow. I told her I'd have to check with you."

Surprise slapped Matt. "Then you agree you're safer not going to Wolf Hollow Community."

Lorie nodded. "Anyone who knows my habits would know that that's my home church. But really, I'm not sure going to a different church would be enough. I don't want to take danger with me wherever I go, so I'm wondering whether I shouldn't stay home and watch a sermon on television."

Matt considered a moment. If church meant as much to

Lorie as it did to him, he didn't want to deprive her of it. "No need to go to that extreme. We can attend my family's church. As long as you're with me, you should be safe."

"You wear a sidearm to church?"

"Keep it under your hat, but yes, I do."

Lorie's eyes twinkled. "How can I keep it under my hat if it's under your arm?"

Matt laughed as Lorie claimed another small piece of his heart. "I wish you'd come back to Dainger County sooner."

A sad look crossed her face. "So do I."

Matt could have kicked himself for reminding her of why she was here, but the damage was done. He'd have to see whether he could cheer her up again while keeping her out of harm's way.

Once she was done with breakfast and he'd drained the last of his coffee, Matt made himself scarce as Lorie called her insurance agent to tell him the bad news. As he walked back to the main house, his cell phone rang. He had it halfway to his ear before he realized he hadn't checked Caller ID.

"MacGregor."

"Hey, Matt, it's Owen."

Matt froze, one foot still in the air. He hadn't spoken to his former friend ever since that heartbreaking conversation where he and Lorene had admitted to Matt that they were in love. He forced himself to breathe, to answer normally. "Owen. What can I do for you?" Slowly he lowered his foot to the ground.

"I—look, there's no easy way for me to say this. Lorene's dying."

The world came to a standstill. Lorene's Facebook page flashed before Matt's eyes. *Thanks for praying.* Was *that* what she'd meant?

"Did you hear me? Matt?"

Matt found his voice. "Dying?"

"Cancer. Stage four. We've tried everything, but it's still growing. I know I betrayed your friendship and stole your girl, but it's too late to do anything about that now. Lorene—we both want to make peace with you. It's something we should have done a long time ago."

The scab over Matt's heart ripped off, letting the festering mess boil to the surface.

"Owen, I can't talk right now. I'm on a case, and it's life and death."

A strangled sob came over the line. "This is life and death, too, Matt…don't you see? Lorene doesn't want to die without knowing you forgive her. Forgive both of us."

Lord, what should I do? Of course, he knew the answer—he was supposed to forgive, to let go of the past and tell Owen that he didn't hold any grudge. But he couldn't say that. Not now. Maybe not ever. The feelings of hurt, betrayal and humiliation had been so strong that he couldn't quite bring himself to let them go.

"I'll call you, Owen, I promise. The minute this case is over."

"But Matt—"

"That's the best I can do. Take it or leave it."

Owen sounded like a broken man. "I hope when you call back it isn't too late."

Matt ended the call and shoved the phone down to the very bottom of his pocket. Why now?

I can't take this right now, Lord. I have to protect Lorie.

Matt stalked into the kitchen of the main house, letting the screen door slam behind him.

"Ooh, what's got you all hot and bothered?"

Matt glared at Sandy, who immediately backed away, both hands in the air.

"Don't shoot, big brother. I'm not armed."

Was he acting that badly?

"Sorry. Pray for Lorene, okay? Owen just called."

"What's wrong?"

Then, with his heart still oozing, he sank down at the kitchen table and told her everything. If he was going to be able to provide proper protection for Lorie Narramore, he had to heal this open sore.

To cheer me up. That's why he's here. Lorie glanced at Matt from time to time as she threaded through the over-stuffed aisles of the outlet store where they'd gone after buying three new cat carriers at the pet store.

She always shopped by herself or, rarely, with Mom, who'd rather be dragged backward through the goal posts at Daingerville High than to go shopping. Having an audience was different.

Not that he seemed like much of an audience. Matt seemed—distracted. That couldn't be a good thing. What had happened while she was calling the insurance company? He'd been fine when he left. Now, even though he kept a watchful eye on her, the distance between them had widened into a chasm.

The store was always crowded on a Saturday, and today was no exception.

Lorie found a dress for Sunday, a silk blouse and a pair of slacks for work. Her total came to $35, which would ordinarily have made her extremely happy. Today it meant nothing. Matt's distance affected her more than she wanted to admit. Even when Matt asked the name of her favorite shoe store, she sensed his withdrawal.

As he started to park the silver Nissan Maxima he'd told her was for taking guests places, Matt peered at the rearview mirror. "Sorry, Lorie. It looks like you'll have to make do with the shoes you have."

"What's wrong?"

"We're being followed."

Lorie's stomach turned inside out. At least, that's what it felt like.

"When did you notice?"

"When we left the outlet store. I've tried to lose him several times, but the way he keeps turning up, I've got to wonder whether he put a tracking device on my car."

Lorie clutched the armrest. "What'll we do now?"

"Drive to the sheriff's office."

Lorie nodded.

Matt took off down Fortieth Street and headed toward the highway that would take them out of West Bluff and back to Daingerville.

Lorie glanced in the mirror. Sure enough, a tan sedan maintained a steady distance.

Matt activated his phone remote, dialing the office. "Hey, Pat, we're being followed. Late-model Lexus sedan, tan, smoked glass. I don't have a plate on him. No front plate decoration."

Lorie listened as she kept an eye on the car behind them. It wasn't attempting to pass them, just keeping pace. As the dispatcher continued speaking into Matt's earpiece, Lorie lost track of the conversation. Her heart pounding, she silently cried out.

Lord, my life is out of control. Please keep us safe.

Matt spoke again. "Roger that. Right now we're headed east on Highway 21. I'll turn off on Cedar, southbound. We'll see if he follows."

But the car kept on going when they turned.

"Arkansas plate."

Matt glanced at Lorie. "Could you get the number?"

"Only part of it. XGY 1 something."

Matt repeated to Pat what Lorie told him.

"Right. I'll meet him there." He touched his earpiece and disconnected the call.

"They're putting out the alert. They should catch the guy and let us know what he was after."

"This is too dangerous. I should leave town."

"And do what? Run? That's no way to live. Besides,

here you have a support system. If you went elsewhere, who would you have for backup?"

It was a good question. Running was low on Lorie's list of plans. She needed to choose her options wisely.

"I don't have the money or the temperament for a life on the run. I just wish—"

"What?"

She couldn't tell him she wished she'd met him under better circumstances. Even if he was a lawman, he was starting to make her believe in opening her heart again. Now that it was too late.

Lorie was thinking so hard that she jumped a foot when her cell phone rang. She swallowed a lump of panic at the unidentified number on Caller ID.

"I don't recognize this number."

Matt held out his hand for the phone. A moment later, he answered it.

"Yes?"

Lorie held her breath, and let it out in a rush when Matt's face cleared.

"It's George—Chief Kershaw, of the fire department— wanting to ask you some questions about the explosion." Matt punched a button and activated the phone's speaker before he gave it to her again and put both hands back on the steering wheel. "Go ahead, George."

"Ms. Narramore, I wanted to let you know what we've determined. The explosive device was rigged to go off the minute the locks were activated. Judging from the level of sophistication, I think we're not dealing with our local troublemakers. You didn't notice anyone hanging around your car?"

"No, sir. I was so busy at work, I never even left the library yesterday. Jen brought in chow mein from Yen's for lunch."

A sigh issued from the phone. "It figures. Well, it didn't hurt to ask. Wish I had better news for you, ma'am, but you can tell your insurance company they can send some-body to look at the pieces whenever they've a mind to."

"Thank you, Chief."

Matt punched off the speaker and exchanged a few more words with Chief Kershaw, which made no sense to Lorie. Her mind was still on what the fire chief had said.

A sophisticated device.

As if she hadn't known the cartel had found her.

Breakfast suddenly felt as if she'd eaten a load of bricks.

If the cartel wasn't stopped, she'd never be safe again.

TEN

When they arrived at the courthouse, Matt led Lorie straight to his tiny office.

"I didn't realize you had an office of your own."

Matt waved a hand at the chair in front of his desk. "Have a seat."

Lorie sank into a chair, looking defeated. "Now what?"

"I want to go over the files with you. Tell me what they don't say."

Lorie closed her eyes. Matt knew it had to be painful even thinking about what had happened back in California, let alone going over the court documents, police reports and news stories. He wished he didn't have to put her through it, but if he was going to get to the bottom of whoever was out to destroy her life, he'd need her help.

And Your help, Lord. Please don't let me hurt her any more than I have to. Even though I'm hurting right now. A picture of Owen and Lorene entered his mind. *And please be with Lorene and Owen. Help me forgive them.*

After a moment, during which Lorie may have also been praying, she opened her eyes. "I'm ready."

Matt turned the monitor in her direction. "Where do you want to begin?"

"Start with the police report. It was the worst, aside from the news coverage."

Matt knew what she meant. The crime-scene photos

were explicit, gory, merciless. The crime-scene photographer had documented the body from every angle, along with the blood spatter, and the bullet hole in the wall next to the ornate framed mirror. Even more painful were the photos of Lorie being led out of the Hotel Del Coronado in handcuffs. Links to the various television stations had video clips of assorted pieces of Lorie's life, the invasion of every moment they could steal.

"I never read everything they had, of course, even though my lawyer tried to get transcripts. Part of me didn't want to read it all. I couldn't believe I'd actually killed a man."

"It isn't easy. No two ways about it."

Lorie looked deep into his eyes. He could read her expression, the shared pain. He wanted to make it go away. Maybe if he told her his story…

"I was on administrative leave for two weeks after I was forced to take out a bank robber. I had to do a lot of heavy soul-searching. Even though you *know* you had no other choice, it still haunts you."

A tear trickled down the left side of her face. "You do understand."

Matt nodded.

Lorie brushed away the tear, leaving a wet streak on her face. "That was the hardest part. The fact he'd never get a chance to trust the Lord, to stop hurting people, to make things right. That I took that chance away from him."

Matt reached out and laid a hand on one of hers. "What I eventually had to do, aside from forgiving myself, was remember if I hadn't stopped that bank robber, he would have shot and killed several others. He'd already critically wounded a pregnant teller."

"Oh." Her voice was filled with pain. "Did she live?"

"Yes, and her baby, too. No thanks to the robber. In your case, you not only stopped a drug lord from killing his girlfriend, but put a huge hole in his drug dealings. No telling how many lives you may have saved by keeping them from getting hooked on drugs."

Tears filled Lorie's eyes. "I tried to look at it that way, but I only ended up feeling like a vigilante. I'm not a cop or a Fed. I'm just a librarian who got in over her head. I don't want to be thought of as the woman who stopped a drug cartel."

Maybe that was the problem. She *had* stopped a cartel, and now they were out for blood.

Lorie developed a sick headache looking at the files the Coronado P.D. had sent Matt. At one point, she almost lost breakfast, but Matt gave her a peppermint.

While it had all been happening she'd been prevented from hearing too much about the unfolding case. However, she'd read as much as she could stand immediately afterward, when she'd returned to her job, and people had started treating her differently. Most of the staff had called her a hero, but some of the library patrons were actually afraid of her. As if while putting books back in the stacks or helping out with the computers she was armed and dangerous....

When it had become too unbearable, despite prayer, she'd been led to move back home.

Now, scanning through the information on Grayson Carl, she realized she hadn't known the half of his illicit activities. Many things hadn't come to light until months later, long after she'd stopped reading about the case. Once he was dead, hidden evil crawled up out of the woodwork like so many termites. Connections with Colombia. Rumors of ties to a network that included not only drugs but arms sales to prohibited countries. She'd taken out a kingpin without realizing she was doing anything except defending herself and another woman.

"This is horrible."

Matt reached across the desk and patted her hand. "I

wish there were something I could do to make it easier for you."

Lorie bit her lip to keep from crying. "Yeah. Me, too."

"There isn't much more. Do you want to keep at it, or stop?"

"Let's get it done. I wish I could forget it ever happened, but obviously someone hasn't forgiven me." How could she tell him how afraid she was? How did fear fit in with her faith?

"You know, there are a few Bible verses I always remember when I'm in tough situations."

Was he reading her mind?

"Which ones?"

"One of my favorites is 'What time I am afraid, I will put my trust in Thee. I have put my trust in the Lord God. I will not fear what men can do unto me.'"

Lorie blinked away tears. "Sometimes that's easier said than done."

"I know. It's a lot easier to trust when things are going well. Times like now? Not so much." He fixed her with a warm gaze. "But you know what? I think you can do it."

Lorie relaxed in the chair. "Yes. You're right." She took a deep breath and let go of the panic for the first time in three days. Or maybe even longer. Deep down, had the panic ever really left, or had she just learned how to cover it well enough to fool herself?

Her eyes closed.

Lord, thank You for Matt. Thank You that I didn't get someone on the case who would have believed I was guilty of murder because a man died at my hands, even though there were extenuating circumstances. Thank You for this peace.

As Matt watched Lorie pray, more of his heart melted. After all she'd been through, she could have been hardened beyond repair. Instead, she was a sweetheart. God had been gracious.

After a couple of minutes, he heard a gentle snore. Bless her heart, she'd dozed off. It was an honor he didn't think he deserved. Not with the congealed lump of unforgiveness he still carted around on his shoulders. His prayer to be able to forgive Lorene and Owen hadn't worked yet. Deep down, he realized he didn't *want* to forgive them. Somehow, that had to change.

He switched off the ringer on his desk phone. His cell phone was already on "vibrate" only. If Lorie could sleep in the middle of the station, in an uncomfortable chair, he'd let her.

Matt scrolled through the rest of the information in the file, looking for anything that might be a clue as to who was trying to kill Lorie.

A few names occurred in the Grayson Carl file, connections who had since been linked with trafficking. They were based primarily in the Californias, U.S. *and* Baja, but hit men could fly anywhere.

That sparked another thought. Matt checked his email. He'd heard back from several of the airlines, with passenger lists. He scanned them, but saw no names connected to the Orgulloso cartel. He downloaded the files to a database where he could do a better job of comparing them.

If someone had driven in, his job would be a little harder. He added a note to send a BOLO out on any plate from California, to stop and check identities. That wouldn't make the tourists happy, but Dainger County didn't get a lot of those from California, since it wasn't on the path of the Interstates and wouldn't be until I-49 was completed.

The light flashed on his phone. Line 1. Matt picked it up as quietly as he could.

"MacGregor."

"Everything okay? Why are you speaking so softly?" His sister's voice was louder than his was.

"Lorie fell asleep in my guest chair. She needs the rest."

"Oh." Sandy lowered her voice. "Well, we've got the prayer chain going for Lorene and Owen. And for you, too."

Matt swallowed the lump that rose in his throat at the mention of Lorene. "Thanks." God knew he needed the prayer. From what Owen had said, they both needed it, too. He wished he could pray for them, but every time he tried, their betrayal rose up and blocked him.

"Tell Lorie the rest of us are getting anxious to meet her."

Another thought occurred to Matt. "What's our guest list like at the moment?"

From the clicking he heard, she was seated at the monitor, probably either in the main lobby or in the office.

"A couple from Minnesota, two families from Northwest Arkansas, a family from Utah, and newlyweds from West Bluff. With Lorie in Cabin 7, we have three vacancies."

"Do me a favor. If anybody tries to make a reservation and gives a California address, put them off."

"You don't mean lie and tell them we don't have a vacancy, do you?" His sister sounded appalled.

"No."

"Because if word got out that we'd started turning people away for no good reason, we'd lose business hand over fist. Besides, I won't lie."

"If anyone from California calls, ask if they can put it off till next week. If they ask point blank whether we have any vacancies, tell them that we do, but we have a—" No, he couldn't have them say there was a situation, because the news might leak out that he was keeping someone in protective custody. "Tell them you'll have to check, and then call me before you rent them a cabin or a room in the lodge, okay?"

"Sure. Is this about Lorie?"

Sandy always had been too perceptive.

"Yes. Someone in California may have sent a hit man after her."

"That's terrible. When she wakes up, tell her I'm praying for her, and I can't wait to meet her. Jim said she's sweet."

Matt looked over at Lorie, her sun-streaked brown hair tumbled over her face, her stomach gently rising and falling with every breath.

"Jim doesn't know the half of it."

Lorie stirred.

"She's waking up."

"I'll let you go, then. Bring her to the family dining room for dinner."

"Yes, Chief."

"Oh, you!"

Sandy rang off, and Matt replaced the receiver as softly as he could.

Lorie blinked and took a deep breath. Matt watched her hunch her shoulders and then stretch. It was beautiful.

Lorie sat up straight. "I'm sorry. I think I must have fallen asleep."

"No problem. You needed the rest."

"Was I out long?"

"About ten minutes."

"I hardly ever do that. Doze off, I mean. During the day."

Matt reassured her again that it was fine.

"Did you find anything else?"

"A few more links to organized crime. Grayson Carl was no loss to society. Since you're awake, let me make a couple of calls."

Lorie nodded.

Matt left a short and cryptic message about the case on the sheriff's cell phone. A moment later he phoned the duty desk and requested the BOLO.

Lorie was watching him when he hung up. "You think someone may have driven out here from California to do this to me?"

"It's a possibility."

"Great. Now I have to be afraid of my favorite license plate."

"Hey, Arkansas has great plates!"

Her eyes twinkled. "I know. I'm looking forward to one of the Diamond State plates. What do you think?"

"I thought you'd go for the 'Read' plate with the stack of books on it."

The smile that lit her face was worth the comment. "That's not a bad idea."

"Let's go. The family is waiting lunch on us."

Lorie stood and collected her purse.

Matt followed her out his office door. Getting a "Read" plate was a good idea, but letting himself get attached to Lorie until the conclusion of this case was a very bad plan. He had to pull back now, for both their sakes. Owen's news had affected his reasoning enough. If his heart became any more involved with Lorie, he was liable to make mistakes. And if he wasn't thinking clearly, and someone succeeded in killing her, he would never get over it for the rest of his life.

There was only one little problem with that decision.

His heart was already involved.

Lorie was quiet on the drive back out to the Rob Roy Ranch, thinking about what Matt had said about dinner with the family. Matt's brother Jim didn't seem too scary, but facing the rest of the family in their own dining room was a daunting prospect. If only she'd met Matt under different circumstances. Say, at church in the singles department. Or at her favorite bookstore in West Bluff…

"Everything okay?"

"Hmm?" Lorie looked over at Matt.

"You sighed."

"Oh. Sorry." She couldn't tell him what she'd been thinking. It would sound like she wished she could have a life with him. Even if that were the case, it could never happen. Not since he knew she'd killed a man, even if that man had been a monster in disguise.

"Still tired?"

His voice was so tender that Lorie shivered.

"It must be a reaction to the last few days."

"Don't worry. We'll be back at the ranch soon and get some dinner in you."

Dinner, as in lunch. Lorie smiled. It had taken her a long time in California to get used to lunch for dinner and dinner for supper. Since she was back in the South, it was taking just as long in reverse.

"Does everybody know why I'm staying there?"

"Yup. Don't let it bother you. I've stashed witnesses at the ranch before."

"Oh."

Why was that notion so disturbing? Did she want to be the only person he'd ever helped? She was being silly and selfish.

The humid summer air was heavy with the scent of pine and wildflowers as they drove the last three miles to the ranch.

Finally, Matt drove through the gates and around to a house she hadn't noticed last night. It was behind the lodge, a few hundred yards away.

"This is the old family house. It was built in 1866 to replace the cabin the Union burned during the War, and added onto up until about 1890."

"Do you all live here?"

Matt shook his head as he opened his door. "We did growing up, but each of us has our own place now. I live in town, but I still have my rooms here. When I retire, I'll probably move back out here to the ranch. There's enough acreage to go around."

Matt opened Lorie's door and gave her a hand out. She was almost getting used to the warm electricity she felt every time they touched. Almost.

The front door opened and a woman stepped out onto the wide porch.

"You must be Lorie. I'm Sandy, Matt's sister. It's so nice to meet you!"

When they reached the top of the stairs, Sandy engulfed Lorie in a hug, which surprised and gratified her.

"Come on in and meet everybody. Dinner's about ready."

"Thank you. It's nice to meet you, too." The words could have been meaningless, but Lorie felt as though if she'd met Sandy under different circumstances, they would probably have been friends at once. She hoped they could be, anyway, despite her current circumstances.

"Who's manning the desk?"

Sandy glanced at Matt. "Terry. I filled her in on your instructions."

"Oh. Okay." He looked at Lorie. "You won't be meeting my niece Terry right now, but you're probably stuck with everybody else."

Sandy laughed. "Now, what a thing to say! Isn't he terrible?"

"I hadn't noticed."

"There's nobody like family to malign your character." Matt gave Lorie a slow smile that sent her interior into a tizzy.

"Who else knows you so well?" Sandy led the way through the old-fashioned living room into the dining room, which, like the one in Lorie's old house, was attached to the kitchen. "Here, let me introduce you."

It wasn't quite a bewildering mob, but as Sandy introduced her to "my husband, Gene, our daughter Missy,

Jim you've met already, Jim's wife, Alana, their children Billy and Lila, our brother Rick, our sister Clara, our sister Henny-short-for-Henrietta, and our baby brother, Jake," Lorie felt as though her head was spinning.

"And I'm Lorie, Matt's current case."

"Oh, you're a case all right." Jake had a heartbreaker's grin.

Another brother chimed in. "And I'm guessing he's got a case on you."

"Rick!"

"Now, Matt, don't get all bent out of shape. She's a pretty lady. And not nearly as geeky as she was in high school."

"Yeah, if you don't want to date her, how about giving your little brothers a recommendation?"

Lorie felt the tension draining from her. Now she remembered Ricky MacGregor, class clown.

When Jim prayed over the meal, the heavy weight of fear in Lorie's heart lifted.

"Lord, bless this food, the hands of those who prepared it, and bless our guest, Lorie. Give us all the strength we need from it, and make us be a blessing to those around us, in Jesus's name. Amen."

Lorie blinked away tears. "Thank you."

Jim just nodded.

Only one problem came to mind: if Lorie became truly comfortable here at the ranch with these wonderful people, she might forget to be cautious. And that would put not only her, but all of them, at risk.

ELEVEN

Matt tried to watch Lorie surreptitiously as her plate was filled with corn pudding, fried chicken, salad, mashed potatoes and gravy, but she caught him looking and smiled. His sisters and sisters-in-law drew her into conversation and made sure Lorie didn't feel left out. The kids clustered at one end of the large mahogany table, the grown-ups at the other.

He could get used to having Lorie's gentle presence among them. He imagined her at the small dinette in his kitchen in town. She would light up the whole house.

Pain clutched at his heart as he remembered the plans he and Lorie—Lorene—had made. He'd wanted to make *her* his whole life, and see where that had gotten him! No, now was not the time to be thinking about Lorie Narramore as anything more than a case. Maybe it never would be time.

"I got a liberry card." Billy gave Lorie a snaggletoothed grin.

"Me, too." His sister elbowed him. "I saw you at the library before, Miss Narramore."

Why didn't she remember?

"Mrs. Jen checked out my books for me."

Of course. Whew. They hadn't actually had a meeting that she'd forgotten. With so many patrons, it was hard to keep them straight out of context, and she'd been greeted many times in the grocery store by familiar faces whose names she couldn't recall.

"You're welcome in the library anytime."

"I'm glad." Alana handed Lorie a plate of hot scratch biscuits. "I was afraid they'd turn into little computer geeks and never open a book, but I got to them early."

Jim laughed. "More likely to have turned into little cowhands here on the ranch."

"That, too." Alana set down the plate. "I'm a teacher at Flavius Holt Elementary, so I try to make sure my students get the best of all worlds, not just technology, in the classroom."

"That must be a challenge."

"It is, but I love it."

"Do you ride?" Rick asked.

"No." Lorie felt the disappointment in the room, but most of it came from Matt. "I never had the chance growing up, and then it was too late. We didn't have the money, either. Mamaw and Papaw had chickens and a few cows, but no horses. I think Papaw was going to get me a pony, but he had a heart attack when I was nine, and after that…"

"Did he die?" Lila's sky-blue eyes were wide.

"Yes."

"Is he with Jesus?"

Lorie nodded, and she felt another tear slide out the corner of her right eye. "Yes, honey. He's with Jesus. That's my biggest comfort, knowing I'll see him and Mamaw again."

"We lost our memaw." Missy spoke directly to Lorie for the first time. "I miss her so much."

"I miss mine, too."

"Are you coming to church with us tomorrow?" Billy shoved half a honey-and-butter-slathered biscuit in his mouth.

"I don't know."

"I hope so." Lila smiled. "We got a real nice church."

"So do I."

"Where do you go?" Sandy asked.

"Wolf Hollow Community Church, but since it's so far from here…maybe I could go with y'all tomorrow."

Matt spoke up. "We'd love to have you."

Lorie looked at Matt and wondered whether he meant for church, or if they'd love to have her in their lives. Could she deal with that?

It was too soon to tell.

After lunch, the family scattered. Jim and Rick told Matt they were planting the back forty today. Jake was off to take a few dudes on a trail ride.

Matt led Lorie back outside to the car. It was so peaceful here. She couldn't imagine why anyone who lived here would want to work anywhere else.

"Why did you go into law enforcement?"

Matt looked surprised as he opened her car door for her. "You mean, instead of settling down and ranching with my family?"

"Something like that."

"I wanted to make a difference. To help people who needed me."

"Didn't your family need you?"

"Yes, but in a different way. Besides, once they found out my heart wasn't in giving riding lessons to city kids, they told me to follow my dream."

Matt got into the car, and they drove the half mile to the cabins in silence.

"I don't know what made me become a librarian. I've always loved books, of course, but I thought I might work in a bookstore, or be an editor."

"You never thought about writing?"

Lorie laughed. "Not with the English courses I took. They made it seem like work. All that syntax and grammar and dissecting themes. The writing exercises I took in college made me able to write good essays, but I guess I don't have the novelist gene in me. I get my imagination fix by reading the works of others."

Matt opened the door to Lorie's cabin, and Colleen bounded out to greet them, the neck cone framing her face.

"She's looking better today."

Lorie nodded as she petted the collie. "I pray she heals soon, and that nothing opens her wound back up. At least it's where she'll have trouble scratching it."

"We should drive back out to your place and see if we can find the cats."

A pang of joy shot through Lorie's heart. "That's thoughtful of you."

"I'll bring a camera and get more photos of the evidence. Then we'll see if there's anything left to salvage."

Matt's words tore through Lorie. Most of her memories of Mamaw and Papaw were tied up in that house, in that land. Last night, she'd been in too much shock to take in specifics. Part of her dreaded seeing all the damage in the clear light of day, but she knew that Matt was right. She needed to get out to the farm and go through things.

As they inched up the gravel driveway to the house in Wolf Hollow, it was hard to see that any destruction had been done. Whoever their perp was, he'd made sure nothing showed from outside on the road. At least it showed he wasn't trying to leave a message for anyone but Lorie.

"It doesn't even look damaged." Lorie echoed Matt's thoughts.

"We'll need to get a locksmith out here."

"I'll call my cousin's husband, Ike, again. He replaced the window and the door lock at the library for me."

"Good idea."

The front door was still secure. The perp had broken in through the kitchen, and the chair they'd wedged under the door before they left last night was still in place.

In daylight, everything looked worse. Not one item appeared to have been left in its original spot.

"Nice place you've got here."

Lorie laughed.

"No, I mean it. The old house has good bones. What was it, a farmhouse?"

"Yes. It was homesteaded in the 1850s, and then Mamaw and Papaw put in electricity and running water when they bought it back in the 1950s."

"Well? Septic tank?"

Lorie nodded. "The only bad part is when the lights go off, I lose the water. However, I don't know if you noticed in the kitchen, but I had a hand pump reinstalled."

"I did notice. I wondered."

"The lights go out too often to suit me. I'm a city girl, remember."

"A city girl with country roots."

"The best of both worlds." Lorie stood beside the overturned sofa. "If you help me, I think we can put this upright again."

Matt put his muscle into it, and they pushed the sofa against the south wall. "There you go, Dobbin. Good as new."

"I'm thankful they didn't slash him to pieces." Lorie patted the sofa as if it were another pet. "That would have been too much."

"At least the piano looks all right."

The old upright's crocheted Victorian piano scarf lay askew, half on and half off, giving the piano the air of a drunken floozy. The glass oil lamp that used to sit on it had been overturned. Lorie wrinkled her nose at the odor of scented lamp oil rising from the soaked carpet.

"You'll need to clean that." Matt picked up the lamp. "At least it didn't break."

"I'm glad."

"How many things can you find to be glad about here, Pollyanna?"

"Hmm. That's a hard one, but here goes. One, I wasn't here when they broke in and trashed my place. Two, my lamp isn't broken. Three—" she straightened the piano scarf "—they didn't steal the piano. Four, Dobbin's all right. How's that?"

"A good start." Matt snapped his fingers. "I forgot to take more pictures. Be right back."

He ran out to the car and fetched the camera.

When he returned to the living room, he found Lorie standing by a large framed reproduction of *Christ in Gethsemane*. He'd last seen it hanging over the fireplace.

"They broke the frame."

The ornate gilded plaster was cracked. Several pieces had fallen onto the native stone hearth. Plaster dust coated everything in the vicinity.

"How old was it?"

"It belonged to my great-grandparents. I think it was a wedding present, so it must date from about 1919. Now it's ruined."

Matt wanted to offer to buy her a new one, but it wouldn't be the same. "Maybe it can be repaired."

Lorie nodded, but he could tell her heart wasn't in it.

"Let me get some pictures."

"Be my guest. I'll go outside and look for the cats." The screen door squawked and slammed, and a moment later, Matt heard her calling the cats by name.

Matt made his way through the house, snapping photos, taking measurements, and in general following up on what the CSI team had done. He'd worked crime scenes often enough to know what to do and how to do it.

Lorie reappeared in the kitchen doorway with the three cat carriers.

"Is it okay to fill the cats' dishes with stuff from the kitchen?"

Matt followed Lorie into the kitchen, where all the cupboards had been emptied. Dishes littered the floor, some broken, others helter-skelter on top of the shards. Seeing it like this fueled an angry fire. Destruction for destruction's sake always did.

"Wait a few minutes, okay?"

Lorie nodded. "May I remove our booby trap?"

"Yes. See if you can remember where it was before we moved it last night."

Lorie picked up the heavy Rococo dining chair and laid it on its side in the pattern of spilled rice and flour, then moved out of Matt's way.

He photographed everything. As he did a circuit of the room, taking enough photos to make a 360-degree collage, he spotted canned cat food next to a box of kitty kibble.

"I've got what I need in here. Don't use the kibble, in case they poisoned it. The cans should be all right." Setting the chair upright again, he handed Lorie the broom and picked up the dustpan. "We need to get this clear before we try to feed the cats." She'd been through enough. Matt didn't want her cats to be harmed.

Lorie swept up all the kibble and other spilled staples she could see and, with Matt's assistance holding the dustpan, deposited the mess in the trash can.

"Thanks. That ought to be safe. I only hope they didn't eat any already."

Lorie picked up three cat dishes from the floor and ran water in them before taking cans to the can opener. Before she opened the first one, she opened the window over the 1950s-era white metal sink.

"Maybe they'll hear the can opener. It usually works."

The roar of the motor from the can opener was loud enough to bring in more than three little cats. It could have called in wolves from the wild.

"You ever consider replacing that?"

Lorie turned to look at him. "What? Mamaw only

bought it in 1978. It's still perfectly good." Her laughter
sent warmth through Matt's veins. He ignored it.

"What did you do with your stuff when you moved back
from California?"

"Sold most of it at a garage sale. My friends helped me.
I gave away a bunch of it." She smiled. "Although I must
admit, if I'd remembered how bad this old thing was, I
would have brought my own can opener." She placed their
dishes into the cat carriers, hoping it would attract them,
since the vandals had destroyed their familiar ones.

Three cats appeared at the screen door and loudly demanded entry.

"There you are! You girls scared me last night, you
know that?"

Lorie passed between the dining room table and the
sideboard to push open the screen door. The cats, a cal-
ico, an orange tiger-kitty and one white cat with a gray
tabby tail and ears streaked into the kitchen and straight
to their bowls.

Matt quickly helped Lorie fasten the carrier doors before the cats could change their minds.

"Typical felines. Just want a meal."

Lorie looked at Matt. "Don't you like cats?"

"Wouldn't want to do without them. Ours live in the
barn and keep the mice from getting out of control."

The house phone rang. Lorie started.

Matt spoke before the second ring. "Do you have a
speakerphone?"

Lorie shook her head.

Matt followed her to the living room, where they found
the phone under a chair cushion. Lorie picked it up and
held the receiver out where they could both listen. Her
apple-scented shampoo tickled his brain.

"Hello?"

The voice on the other end was run through some kind
of processor, but the message was perfectly clear.

"*Murderer.*"

* * *

Panic seized Lorie, and she couldn't speak. Matt mouthed the words "Keep him on the line" and punched a few silent numbers on his cell phone.

"Uh." Brilliant. "Who is this?"

"That's unimportant." The processor made the speaker sound like a robot. *"You stole a life. Now yours is forfeit. But first, I'm taking away everything you love. And everyone. Starting with your parents."*

Click.

"No!" Lorie met Matt's eyes. "Were you able to trace it?"

Matt shook his head. "Not long enough. We'll get the records from the phone company."

"Matt, he's threatened my parents!"

Matt set his camera on the sofa and without analyzing his motives pulled Lorie into his arms.

"We'll put them in protective custody."

"But—"

"It's all right." His arms tightened around her.

Lorie buried her face in his shoulder, her arms wrapping around him, holding on as if the contact would keep her world from falling apart.

"I'll call the department, have them send somebody out there at once. What's their address?"

Lorie pulled back and looked at him. "What if my attacker bugged the house? What if I tell you the address, and he goes to kill my parents?"

"All right. Let's lock up here. We'll call from the car."

"Thanks for not thinking I'm paranoid." She tried to smile and failed.

"If I'd had a week like yours, I'd be paranoid, myself."

Matt helped Lorie carry the cats to the Nissan and secure them in the backseat. Once in the car, Matt drove away before calling the department. Lorie hoped they

weren't being followed by someone with a field microphone.

*Girl, you've watched too many espionage films. Either
they have one, or they don't. There's nothing you can do
about it but pray.* Why hadn't she thought of that sooner?

*Lord, things are getting out of hand. Please protect
Mom and Dad. Protect Matt. Protect me, too. And please
stop this person before things get any worse.*

As they drove toward West Bluff, Lorie remembered
how safe she'd felt in Matt's arms. Of course, he hadn't
meant anything by it. He had just been comforting her,
keeping her from having hysterics. That was all it was,
wasn't it? It had to be. She hadn't known him long enough
for it to be anything more.

Maybe, when this was all over, if she could let go of her
suspicion of law enforcement…

Lorie sniffed. No sense thinking about the future.
Things were so iffy, she wasn't sure she'd live to see tomorrow. She shoved the thoughts ruthlessly behind a shelf
in her brain.

"City police have sent an officer."

Matt's voice recalled Lorie to the present.

"They won't scare them, will they?"

"Their dispatch told me they were sending Officer Rod-
riguez. He's good. He'll handle it gently."

"Thanks. I want to see them so much, but I'm scared
to get near them for fear someone will harm them. I'm
even scared to call them, afraid I'll give them a heart attack or something."

"Be brave." After a moment, Matt chuckled.

Lorie glanced at him sideways. "What was that for?"

"I'm laughing at me, telling you to be brave. You're one
of the bravest people I know."

"Me, brave? I don't think so." If she felt any less coura-
geous, she'd find a hole and pull it in after her.

"Bravery is just doing what's right in the face of over-whelming circumstances."

"I hadn't thought of it that way." Lorie considered the concept for a moment, but then felt her thoughts drift toward other concerns.

"I wish we could have finished cleaning, but the phone call messed that up. Kind of like the caller messed up the house in the first place."

"I'll call out the family troops. We'll come out in a bunch and go through it together."

"I hate for your family to see the place looking like such a disaster area."

"This was *not* your fault." Matt's words were like a hug.

"I know that with my head, but emotionally is another story. Get enough pictures?"

"I think so. We should be good to go in terms of laying out charges as soon as we round up your assailant."

Lord, please let that be soon!

TWELVE

This case kept getting worse and worse. Every time Matt felt like he was making progress, something came along and muddied the water again. Now someone was threatening not just Lorie but also her family. And he had to find out who before it was everlastingly too late.

When they drove up in front of the West Bluff Police Department, Lorie let out a little squeal.

"Their car is here. They're safe."

"I told you WBPD would look after them."

Matt found a space on the opposite side of the lot from the Narramores' car, but still well within sight of the surveillance cameras. Matt rolled down all the windows so the cats would be safe.

They walked into the updated 1870s stone police station together and stopped at the front desk. Matt flashed his badge. "Deputy MacGregor. Where can I find the Narramores?"

"They're with Lieutenant Buckingham. Second office to the right."

"Thanks."

Matt took Lorie's arm in an old-fashioned gesture of protectiveness and tried to ignore the sense of warmth, of rightness it gave him. At the second door, he released her and tapped twice on the glass.

"Come in."

Matt walked in, Lorie right behind him.

Two seconds later, the emotional reunion made Matt feel superfluous. Amid cries of "Mom!" "Dad!" "Lorie!" "Baby, are you okay?" and hugs, it was a full two minutes before everyone sat down in the lieutenant's office.

Once all the greetings had been exchanged and Lorie introduced to Lieutenant Buckingham, the police officer got down to business.

"What exactly did the man say to you, Ms. Narramore?"

Lorie recounted everything she could recall, and where shock had robbed her of memory, Matt filled in the gaps. Her parents were understandably upset. Matt noticed they seemed to be more afraid for her than for themselves.

"What happens now?" Ben Narramore asked the lieutenant, his glance also including Matt.

"The threat against you and your wife moved the case into our jurisdiction." Lieutenant Buckingham looked over at Matt. "From the sound of things, we could bring in the FBI if we have to. However, I'm always reluctant to call in the Bureau unless there's no other option."

Matt agreed. "So basically, we need to have a powwow with the sheriff and the West Bluff Chief of Police."

"That's my thought." Lieutenant Buckingham sounded stoic.

"I hate to be the cause of so much trouble."

The distress on Lorie's face affected Matt more deeply than he'd expected. When her parents each took her by the hand, he had to fight wishing he were a part of that tight-knit little circle. The notion surprised him. He wasn't ready for love, so why did he find Lorie's family so appealing?

"The best thing will be to stash you someplace safe."

"We can't run off and hide, Lieutenant. We have obligations."

"Ma'am, you also have a daughter who doesn't want to see you get hurt on her account."

"Lieutenant Buckingham is right, Margaret." Ben Narramore reached around Lorie and took his wife's free hand in his own. "The church can get along without us one Sunday, or even more if necessary."

"But what about your job?"

"I'll take some time off."

"You're more than welcome to come out to the ranch." Matt heard the words come out of his mouth before he'd thought about it. It wasn't the best idea. If they were all together, they'd make an easier target.

"I don't want them to find any of us." Lorie looked at Matt, and the question in her eyes was plain. Could he guarantee their safety?

No. Only God could do that. Surely Lorie knew the only safety was in the Lord. Anything else was icing on the proverbial cake.

"It's a judgment call." Buckingham must be looking at it from the law enforcement point of view. "Do you think you can provide adequate protection at Rob Roy Ranch, or should we send them someplace under an assumed name? It would be tricky to get the finances for that approved, but I could give it a try."

Matt thought about it, considering all the wooded areas and open pastureland of the ranch, the tree-covered hills and edges of the mountains. It was excellent hunting country, as the deer they bagged every autumn testified. Would it be just as convenient for hunters with humans as their prey?

"It has a lot of unprotected approaches, but we installed security cameras last year. The main compound is fenced. If Sheriff Sutherland gives me leave to devote my attention to this full-time, and maybe assigns someone else to help out so we have round-the-clock surveillance…"

"If the sheriff doesn't object, we can make sure one of our SWAT-trained officers is available to you, in plain clothes," the lieutenant offered. "I won't send uniforms or patrol cars out of the city. Might as well wave a banner over the ranch if we did that."

Matt nodded. "All right. We'll manage. And in the meantime, we'll all do what we can to track that—um, perpetrator, down and put him away for a long time."

"Sounds like a plan."

"What about clothes?" Mrs. Narramore sounded unhappy.

"Sorry, Mom, I guess we'll have to go shopping."

Margaret rolled her eyes. "Do we have to?"

"It's safer than returning to the house to get anything." They all stood to leave.

"I'll get on the horn with the sheriff." Lieutenant Buckingham shook Matt's hand. "You keep these people safe."

"Count on it."

As they walked out of the police station together, Matt hoped that was one promise he could keep.

Matt examined both cars before he let anyone get into them. He checked for explosive devices, leaks in the brake or transmission lines, even kicked the tires to make certain no one had damaged them to make them leak slowly.

"As far as I can tell, they haven't been tampered with."

He crawled out from under Lorie's parents' car somewhat the worse for wear, but he looked like a hero to Lorie.

Oh, dear. These feelings she was experiencing were totally inappropriate. It had to be an attraction based on the circumstances. Nothing real could happen this fast. Could it? Even if he weren't in law enforcement, now was hardly the time to think about romance. Not with her parents in danger, and the same crazy person who'd already done so much damage at the root of it all.

Matt found a parking place close to Lorie's parents' car at the shopping center. A city police unit pulled in beside them. The blue-uniformed officer rolled down the window.

"Deputy MacGregor?"

Matt nodded.

"Lieutenant Buckingham sent me to keep an eye on the cars so you could guard the Narramores."

Matt smiled. "Thank him for me."

The officer behind the wheel nodded. "Will do."

"I wondered how I was going to be in two places at once."

Matt reached out and took Lorie's hand, as though they were on a date instead of a shopping expedition under guard.

If Mom and Dad noticed, they didn't say anything. They smiled and Dad took Mom's hand in his. The look Dad gave Mom made Lorie wish she had someone who loved her that way. She glanced at Matt.

If only he were anything but a lawman…

Matt watched in amusement as Mrs. Narramore shopped. Lorie was right. Her mother really would rather be doing almost anything else. Mr. Narramore ended up helping her choose some things for herself as well as him, and Lorie picked out half the dresses her mother bought.

"We ought to get you something, too." Lorie looked at Matt, her head tilted to one side, studying him. "You smeared oil and grease all over your clothes when you were making sure nobody'd tampered with our cars."

Matt shook his head. "They'll wash, and I have more at home." Looking to distract her from the idea of spending her money on him, he asked if they needed anything else.

"We should stop by the shoe store. I still need something decent, and Mom and Dad don't have any spares, either."

Proudfoot's Heel-To-Toe carved a large footprint of mall space. Matt preceded the Narramores into the footwear emporium, his eyes marking off the distances between men's and women's departments.

The stacks of shelves climbed much higher than Matt liked. Almost anyone could hide in the aisles.

One woman with expensive, upswept blond hair had a stack of boxes in front of her as she tried on a pair of extreme, zebra-stripe platform spike heels. Matt turned to glance at Lorie and was surprised at the smile on her face.

"Don't tell me you like them."

Lorie leaned in closer and murmured in his ear. "You mean those Frankenshoes? No way."

Matt swallowed a chuckle as a sales assistant, wearing sensible trainers, headed in their direction.

As Lorie and her mother followed the assistant, Ben Narramore tapped Matt's shoulder.

"What's your take on all this?"

The moment of lightness faded as the seriousness of the situation hit home again. "We're still looking into everything, but it seems very much as if her troubles have followed her here."

"That's what concerns me, too."

Lorie and Margaret sat down in chairs close to the blonde shoe shopper and waited for the sales assistant.

From the men's section of the store, a face Matt knew well appeared and strode over to the blonde. Matt froze. Leonard Adderson was here?

"What do you think, Lennie?" Blondie stuck out one foot and modeled the zebra stilt.

"It's what you think that matters, baby."

She squealed and threw her arms around his neck, threatening his expensive-looking necktie. At that moment, Adderson spotted Matt's uniform and visibly flinched before he regained his composure.

Ben nudged Matt. "Isn't that the real estate and property-management guy?"

Among other things, including suspected drug mogul. Not that they'd been able to prove anything yet. Matt nodded. "Let's speed this up."

Ben's sharp look told Matt he understood. The two of them ambled toward the Narramore ladies.

"About done, sweetheart?"

Margaret nodded. "These will do."

"I have what I need, too." Lorie put a lid on the shoe box and picked it up.

Adderson fixed Matt with a bland stare. "Afternoon, Deputy."

"Good afternoon, sir." Matt stood still as the well-dressed but dissolute businessman gave him a nod. If only he could prove Adderson was behind the mushrooming number of meth labs in Dainger County.

The blonde and Adderson headed for the cashier. Matt held a hand out, low, to stop Lorie and Margaret from following.

"Let them go. I want some distance between us and them."

Lorie looked a question at Matt. He couldn't answer, not with Adderson still within earshot, but he raised an eyebrow.

"Come on, Mom, let's help Dad find something."

The Narramores turned toward the men's shoe department. Matt saw Adderson watching them as if burning them into his memory. If he'd been tempted to dismiss the real-estate mogul as a possible suspect in Lorie's case, that inclination had just flown out the window.

On the drive to the ranch, Lorie could feel Matt's darkened mood in the atmosphere like an approaching storm. The sun was still shining, just not in Matt's car. Lorie wondered if she'd done something to ruin things. Was he upset by the way she'd been joking earlier? She'd only wanted to forget, for a few minutes, the state of the world in general and her world in particular.

Well, she guessed a few minutes were all she had. Now it was back to reality.

He followed Mom and Dad's car to the lodge and parked. By the time they got out, her parents were already standing next to it, looking all around at the trees surrounding the lodge.

"Isn't this lovely?" Mom took a deep breath of the pine-scented air and smiled. "Why haven't we ever come out here before, Ben?"

"Maybe because it was too close to home?"

"Mom and Dad always have liked long driving vacations," Lorie explained to Matt, "before—"

"Before the trial," Dad finished. "And I'm sure we'll go again. Maybe we can twist your arm to come with us this time, cupcake. We miss having you along for the ride, complaining about how I never stop for anything interesting."

An answer stuck in Lorie's throat. All she could do was nod.

"Come on in. Unless they rented them all out since this morning, we still have two cabins available."

"Can't we share Lorie's?"

"It's only a one-bedroom. I don't think we have any two-bedroom cabins left."

"Oh." Mom sounded disappointed. But then again, she'd also been disappointed when Lorie had decided to renovate Mamaw and Papaw's old place rather than move into the house with them in West Bluff. Considering what happened to the house, she could only be grateful she'd stood firm. She didn't even want to think what the vandal might have done to her parents if they'd been there when the attack took place.

Dad wrapped an arm around Mom's shoulder, and they climbed the porch stairs together. Alana was behind the desk when they entered.

Matt performed brief introductions as close to the desk as possible, and kept his voice low. His sister-in-law followed suit.

"How about Cabin 14, Mr. and Mrs. Narramore?"

"Is that close to Lorie's cabin?"

"Cabin 4 is closer. It's the other option."

Mom smiled. "If it wouldn't be too much trouble, we'd rather be closer to Lorie."

Alana smiled. "No trouble at all."

Lorie wondered whether it actually wasn't any trouble, or whether Alana had simply chosen not to let it be a problem. Either way, Alana handed Dad the key.

"Any new guests?" Matt's tone was casual, but Lorie knew a lot was riding on the answer.

Alana shook her head. "Not since the couple from Pickertown this morning, who took Cabin 12. One attempt to register from the L.A. area, but I put them off. They wanted a week, too."

"I'm so sorry." Guilt washed over Lorie. "It's all my fault. If it weren't for me, you could have rented it and made a lot of money."

"Money's not that important." Alana sounded definite. "Not where there's a life at stake."

"Don't you dare feel guilty," Matt added. "None of this is your fault. Remember that."

"I keep trying."

If how she felt now was any indication, it was going to be a long time before Lorie felt safe and guilt-free.

Seated around the dining table in Lorie's cabin with her and her parents, Matt could see that they were as tight-knit as his own family. How well would an outsider fit into their little unit? Would they embrace a son-in-law, or would he always feel like an unwelcome addition? Of course, that was none of his business, unless the Lord changed his circumstances drastically.

Listening to the three of them chat as they shared glasses of iced tea, Matt leaned back in his chair. Lorie and her mother were doing most of the talking. Ben was sitting back looking as if he was trying unsuccessfully not to worry. Before long, the talk shifted back to their current circumstances.

"But what do I tell my Sunday-school class?"

"You call Dorothy and get her to substitute for you, Mom. The class will understand once we can tell them what's going on. In the meantime, get the prayer chain started. That can only help."

Matt spoke up. "Tell them you need their prayers, but don't go into specifics. And *don't* tell them where you are or how long you'll be away. The first is for your safety, and answering 'I don't know' for the second is nothing but the truth."

"I hope we aren't in for too long a haul."

"Me, too, Dad. I'm sorry about all this."

"You were in the wrong place at the wrong time."

Lorie chewed her lower lip a moment. "You know, I'm not sure about that anymore. God knows everything from beginning to end. I'm not sure but what I was meant to be in that restroom lobby at that moment in time. I can't believe I was meant to kill that man, but I know the Lord's hand was on me."

"And you did save Miss Montoya's life."

Something about that scenario still bothered Matt. Why would the woman leave Lorie to face trial like that, without even testifying on her behalf? It didn't feel right.

Lorie turned to Matt. "So, where do we go from here?"

"Well, first and foremost, we do our best to protect you. Second, we try to catch the person responsible, so none of you are in any more danger."

"I think we need to pray about this."

Ben's quiet assertion resonated with Matt. Matt nodded. Lorie and Margaret held out their hands, and Matt was drawn into their circle in an intimate, spiritual way.

Ben's praying voice was as straightforward as his speaking voice.

"Lord, we're in a mess here. Please give us the grace we need to go through this time of testing. Please protect and show us what to do. Give Matt wisdom and guidance.

Let this person threatening us be brought to justice, and don't let him harm Your children, Lord. We ask this all in the name of Your Son, Jesus. Amen."

Margaret added her two cents' worth to the prayer. "Lord, thank You that we heard of this plot against us before more damage could be done. Thank You for Your protection every day, not just today. You're so good, Lord. Thank You that Lorie is safe. Amen."

Lorie took a breath. "Thank You for Matt, Lord. Please keep him safe, and Mom and Dad."

Lorie squeezed Matt's hand, and for a moment, all conscious thought left him. Then he realized she meant for him to add to their prayer. Whew. This attraction had to stop before he lost control of the situation and the unthinkable happened. He couldn't let Lorie or her parents be killed. Not on his watch. Instantly, he felt a rebuke in his spirit.

"Not on *Your* watch, Lord. Don't let them be hurt on Your watch. And help us to remember we're *always* on Your watch. Thank You. Amen."

Lorie gave him a warm smile. "Thanks, Matt. I really needed that."

She squeezed his hand again, and his brain nearly exploded.

Lord, keep me sane. And if this attraction is from You, please work things out so we can have a future together. If not...

That was the hard part.

If not, he had to let her go.

THIRTEEN

Matt asked Lorie and her parents over to supper with the family, but they turned him down. Lorie hoped the Mac-Gregors would understand.

"Not a problem," Matt assured her. "I'll bring y'all a plate of everything."

"You don't have to do that." Mom was always more polite than practical.

"It's no problem, Mrs. Narramore."

"Please call us Ben and Margaret."

"Thank you."

Matt left, instructing Lorie to lock the door after him and not let anyone else in.

Left alone with her parents, Lorie discovered they had taken a keen interest in Matt.

"That young man likes you."

"Oh, Mom."

"Your mother's right. You should see the way he looks when he's watching you." Dad grinned. "I believe the boy's smitten."

"He's hardly a boy, Dad. He's older than I am. He went through school with Jen."

Dad exchanged a glance with Mom, one of those smiling, parents-know-best looks. The kind Lorie loathed. Especially since they were usually right. That only made it worse.

"It doesn't matter whether he likes me or not."

"You like him, too." Another Mom pronouncement.

"Now is not the right time."

"I know you're going through a lot, but he seems like a nice man."

"You know how I feel about policemen."

"He's not a policeman, he's a deputy." Mom tried unsuccessfully to hide another smile.

Lorie sighed. "I can't handle it, Mom."

Dad reached out and took Lorie by the hand. "You know, cupcake, you can't keep on blaming the entire world of law enforcement for what you experienced in California."

"I know." Lorie swung her hand in her Dad's, the way she had when she was a little girl. "It's just so hard to get past the emotional blockade." Even though they were right. It wasn't fair to blame Matt for every assumption San Diego County law enforcement had made of her guilt. Her cousin Noah worked for the San Diego Sheriff's Department, for pity's sake, and she hadn't taken it out on *him*. But family was different. And she wasn't sure she could let go of all of her fears and defensiveness just because she knew Matt didn't deserve them.

Mom dragged her into a hug. "I'm sorry, sweetie. You know I just want *you* to be happy."

"I'll be happy when all this is over and our lives can go back to normal." *If that ever happens*.

A knock at the door and Matt's voice told them he was back with supper. A delicious aroma assaulted Lorie's senses when she opened the door. "Oh, that smells so good. Come on in."

"Hope you don't mind if I join you. I brought enough for all of us, and I'll feel better keeping an eye on you."

"Of course we don't mind." Mom spoke for all of them. She started getting plates down from the cupboard.

Lorie got flatware out of the drawer. Dad grabbed a

basket of goodies from Matt. This was turning into a pic-nic. Indoors. With her favorite chaperones.

Lord, help me to remember why we're all here. This is about our lives.

Part of her couldn't help wishing, however, that she and Matt were on a nice picnic somewhere, maybe under a tree, with warm sunshine and the sweet scent of honeysuckle in the air. But dwelling on that would be foolish—and letting her mind wander might put her at risk.

"Who's watching to make certain nobody sneaks onto the ranch?"

"You mean besides the security video and the SWAT officer from West Bluff? I called the department. We've got a deputy volunteering to be here on his free time. Then, too, my brothers are no slouches. My sisters and the in-laws, either. If anything were to happen, if someone tried to come onto the property with the intent to do harm, there are plenty of us to see that doesn't happen."

Matt's words gave her a confidence she hadn't felt since the first note appeared.

"I just thought of something."

"What's that?" Dad looked up from the plate of chicken fried steak.

"The harassment started while I was still in San Diego. After I moved back here, it let up for months. I thought it was over. Why now? What changed?"

"Maybe they were letting you have a breather. Letting you think it was over, before this new plan of attack."

Lorie swallowed a bite of potato salad. "I can't imagine who it could be, unless it's someone connected with Carl's operation. Oh, I wish I'd never gone to that gala dinner and auction."

"You didn't have a choice, from what you told your mother and me," Dad said, clearly trying to comfort her.

Lorie shook her head. "It was such a huge event, crawling with media. No excuses, be there or else, unless you're dying."

Lorie swallowed hard. If she hadn't been there, would Carl still be alive? Or would Ms. Montoya have killed him? Would he have killed Ms. Montoya? The story might have had a vastly different ending if she'd had a flat tire and couldn't make it, or had contracted, say, pneumonia. Anything. But as she'd said earlier, she had to believe the events were part of God's plan. A plan that would come clear to her in time—she just wasn't there yet.

"Lorie, are you all right?"

Lorie shook herself. The words finally penetrated after Mom repeated them.

"I will be. This is just one more trial. I pray the Lord will help us through it." If He didn't... No. That didn't bear consideration.

Matt's hand tightened on Lorie's, and something flared in her eyes. Hope?

"Let's finish eating this before it gets cold."

"Are you—"

The phone rang.

Fear flashed across Lorie's face.

"Who knows we're here?"

Matt got up. "I'll answer it." He crossed to the phone and picked up the ancient black receiver.

"Rob Roy Ranch."

But it was only Jim on the phone. "We had a call from Leonard Adderson wanting half a dozen cabins for a weekend party."

"Leonard Adderson?" Matt's voice was louder than he'd have liked. Three heads swiveled to look in his direction. He lowered his voice. "We just ran into him at Proudfoot's in West Bluff."

"All of you?" Jim's question came quick and hard.

"Yup. What did you do?"

"I told him that we didn't have that many vacancies. Also, due to the family nature of the ranch, we couldn't allow him to bring his party here, not without having to remove the other guests, and they had first priority."

"Good thinking. But we'll have to keep a closer eye on things now."

"Yep. Wanted to give you a heads-up."

"Thanks."

Matt rang off and looked back at the Narramores. "Nothing too serious—just a cabin rental request. We turned it down."

"What is it about Adderson you don't like?" Ben had his head cocked to one side. "Aside from his flamboyant lifestyle, I mean."

"The day I met Lorie, I'd narrowly missed making a drug bust. A lead on a meth lab fizzled. The cooks had gotten advance warning and cleared everything out. They were gone before we arrived. We'd put a lot of time into the investigation." He took the three of them in with a look. "I hope I can trust you not to let this go any further. Adderson owned the property where the meth was being made. And he's been tied to multiple other properties associated with drugs before."

Alarm flared in Lorie's eyes. Margaret reached out and took Ben's hand.

"Do you think he's connected with Carl's drug organization? Could he be behind the threats?" Ben's voice was quiet, as if he were concerned someone might be listening at the door.

"From what I can tell, no, but his wanting to rent cabins today, after seeing me with all of you—"

"It does seem a trifle opportune." Margaret squeezed Ben's hand.

"That makes me nervous about staying here." The way Lorie gnawed her lower lip emphasized the statement.

"Try not to worry. The department is keeping him under surveillance. You're safe here."

"What about church tomorrow? I know Mom wanted to go to First."

"If you don't mind, we could go together to Grace Church. It'd be better than going back to Daingerville."

"Is that around here?" Ben asked.

"Yes, about three miles down the road in Preston. My brothers and sisters and family are there every week. I join them when I can, but I'm almost never here."

"Well, you're working." Ben nodded. "Hard to be two places at once, though I'd have done it a few times during my military career if I could have."

Margaret reached out and squeezed Ben's hand. Obviously, they had a good marriage. The same sort Matt wanted for himself one day. The sort he'd kept too busy working since the breakup with Lorene to try to find.

Not that he hadn't had ladies interested in him, especially at his church in town, but somehow, none had ever generated more than a slight interest on his part. Nothing like the connection he felt with Lorie.

Even with her parents sitting here in the same room with them, he felt warmer just being near her.

If this isn't from You, Lord, please let it end well, so we can still be friends.

A memory of Lorene surfaced. The diamond engagement ring glittered on her left hand as she showed it off to their friends. He'd felt so proud then, so happy the head cheerleader had chosen a linebacker instead of the quarterback. So glad she didn't want to wait until they went off to college to get married.

Then his football scholarship to the University of Louisville came through, and suddenly, Lorene didn't want to leave Arkansas. They'd argued about it, to the point where she'd announced she wouldn't marry him unless he changed his mind. It was an uncharacteristic argument. Up to that point, he'd always given her what she wanted, always conceded. This time, however, the school had the Justice Administration degree he needed. He tried reasoning with her, to no avail.

Two nights later, he caught her with Owen, the quarterback, at *their* spot on Lake Cholah. Matt's stomach churned, remembering Lorene's hurried "I can explain" along with Owen's "It's not what you think." Right. *Sure* it wasn't.

Later, she'd tried to stay friends. Matt had cut her off every time she tried to talk to him, had walked away after Lorene shoved his ring into his shirt pocket. He had gone to Kentucky and not looked back, but news of Lorene and Owen's hasty marriage, followed by the birth of their daughter five months later, told him she'd been cheating on him a lot longer than he'd imagined.

"Matt? Is something wrong?" Lorie's voice broke through into his unhappy thoughts.

"I'm okay. Why? Did you hear something?"

Lorie shook her head. Matt was thankful that she didn't *look* like his former Lorie. It was a small blessing. Maybe not so small.

Thank You, Lord, for Your guidance in this situation, and please help us to get out of it safely by Your grace.

Saturday sank into oblivion. They finished the dessert Matt had brought over, a delicious Sacher torte Alana liked to bake.

"Well, I guess we'd better turn in."

Margaret gave Lorie another big hug. "Call us if you need anything."

"You, too, Mom."

"Are you sure you don't want to come and sleep on the couch in our cabin?"

"Mom, I'll be fine."

Watching her parents walk to Cabin 4 with Matt, Lorie felt a sense of foreboding. Colleen whined from the bedroom where she'd been shut in. The cats' displeased meows added to the cacophony.

"Oh, poor things." Lorie opened the door and buried her hands in Colleen's amber-and-white fur as the cats headed for the cozy couch. "You poor baby. Are you feeling better? Huh, girl?"

Colleen responded by licking her hand.

Lorie checked Colleen's bandage. It hadn't worked loose. That was a blessing. The last thing she needed on top of everything else she was going through was for Colleen to get a bad infection.

An attempt to pet the cats was met with disdain on their part. Oh, well. They'd forgive her eventually. She hoped.

After she'd changed into her pajamas, Lorie realized she'd still forgotten to bring anything to read. She picked up the Gideon Bible again and opened it to the front, flipping through the pages. The cadence of Renaissance language, the Elizabethan flavor of the words, made them seem like poetry.

Depth of mercy. Grace. Peace.

Lorie flipped the book open to the back, and thumbed through until she came to "Peace I give unto you. Not as the world giveth, peace give I unto you." Jesus's words gave her comfort. Peace in the midst of storm. That's what it was all about.

Lord, thank You for Your peace. Thank You for this place to shelter ourselves from those who would seek to harm my family and me.

The feeling of peace lasted, and Lorie readied herself for bed. Colleen lay at the foot of the bed again as Lorie tucked herself in and turned out the light.

Despite the sensation of peace, sleep was a long time in coming.

* * *

A knock at the door seemed to come just after Lorie had fallen asleep. But, blinking at the light leaking through the draperies, she realized it must be morning.

"Just a minute."

Lorie threw on a light cotton robe over her pajamas and padded to the door.

Matt stood outside.

"Hope I didn't wake you."

"'I cannot tell a lie,' so I have to admit that you did. But that's okay. I needed to wake up anyway." *After another two hours of sleep, preferably.*

Matt grinned ruefully. "Sorry! I thought you'd want to get ready in plenty of time for Sunday school."

"Sunday school?"

"It's High Attendance Sunday. Say you'll join us so we can drive up the record?"

Lorie rolled her eyes and stifled a yawn. "Okay. As soon as I wake up. Did you talk to my parents yet?"

"Not yet."

Matt nodded as Lorie stretched. "Do you want to come in for some coffee?"

"No, really I came to tell you breakfast will be ready whenever you want it at the house. I'll drive y'all over."

"Mom will say she doesn't want to be a bother." Lorie smothered another yawn. "Talk her into it anyway. She doesn't need to cook this morning."

"Will do." Matt reached out and tweaked a stray curl out of Lorie's face. "Maybe if you splash some water on your face, it'll help you wake up."

"No doubt. Thanks."

Colleen padded to the door and put her nose in Matt's hand. Matt responded appropriately, giving the dog a good scratch behind the ears.

"I'll go get your parents and then I'll be back to drive you to the house."

"Thanks."

Lorie closed the door after him, and then headed for the bathroom to see if a dose of cold water really would wake her.

Matt's cell phone rang as he was heading back to the main house. Seeing Frank's number, he answered at once.

"What's up?"

"An anonymous call came into the station about the Narramore case. Gerhardt alerted me."

Matt froze in place. "Any luck tracing it?"

"Not yet. You're not going to like what was said."

Something cold settled in the pit of Matt's stomach. "Tell me."

"The caller emailed a link to a URL from some crack-pot blog purporting to tie Ms. Narramore to the Orgulloso cartel. He said they'd been using the library system's vehicles to transport black heroin and cocaine from the San Ysidro branch to libraries all over the city."

"Lorie told me about that smear campaign. It's nothing new. The only difference is now, they're not trying to influence the trial, they're just trying to make her look guilty after the fact, so we'll call off the protection. I happen to agree with the jury that she's not guilty, but even if she was, she still has a right to protection. No matter what happened in California, the person threatening her is the one breaking the law now."

"I know—that's why the protection detail is staying in place. Still, if she's keeping things from you, then danger might end up coming from a direction you're not expecting. Just be careful, Matt. I know her father, but I don't really know Lorie."

The words seeped into Matt's soul like poison. What if Lorie *had* been working for the cartel? What if Carl's death hadn't been justifiable homicide? What if she really *had* deliberately assassinated him?

Matt's mind recoiled from the thought. Lorie couldn't be guilty of murder, even though she'd shot and killed the man. It had been accidental self-defense.

Hadn't it?

FOURTEEN

Matt handed Lorie's parents to another deputy once they reached Grace Church. John Douglas was nearing retirement age, and so was a more appropriate fit for the married couples' Adult III class.

Matt went with Lorie to the Adult II class and chose a chair where he could watch the door. He'd have to be sober and vigilant, as the scripture suggested, because it wasn't only his soul he needed to safeguard. It was also Lorie. Whether or not she was guilty of murder, someone was out to destroy her.

Lorie fit into the class as if she'd been born to it. As it happened, Sandy and Jake weren't the only people she knew. When she was through greeting her friends, she turned back to Matt with a questioning look on her face.

"Where's Rick?"

"Watching the desk in case of the guests needing anything. They all take turns having a Sunday."

Lorie nodded. "That makes sense."

The lesson that morning, taught by the pastor's wife, was on how safety is found only in the Lord. Talk about fitting the situation. If Matt hadn't known that the Sunday-school board had planned the lesson in advance, he would have wondered if Edna had engineered it to fit what was going on in their lives.

The glance Lorie exchanged with Matt told him she thought the same thing.

He smiled in a way that he hoped was reassuring, and shrugged his shoulders a tiny bit to show he'd had nothing to do with it. This was strictly the Lord's doing.

The class had a lot of give-and-take. Matt hoped Lorie would have sense enough not to mention what she was going through at the moment, and she didn't disappoint him. Sandy, however, mentioned the Lord was taking care of all of them in a sticky situation, and that He was showing Himself faithful even though things were not the way they should be.

After class, they broke up to go into the sanctuary for the church service. The musicians were tuning their instruments. A violinist, rhythm guitarist, lead guitarist, bass player and drummer formed the complete ensemble. They looked a little silly standing next to the organ, but Matt always enjoyed the music they made when he visited.

After meeting up with Lorie's parents, they agreed to sit on opposite sides of the church. Once again, Matt stationed himself where he could keep watch on the doors. Deputy Douglas did the same, monitoring the set of doors near the senior Narramores.

After church, Matt drove Lorie and her parents back toward Rob Roy Ranch. At Matt's suggestion, Lorie called Ginny Travis to explain she couldn't make lunch this week, but she hoped they'd be able to meet up soon. After a similar call to Ike and Tammy to reschedule their planned supper, they reached the ranch.

The moment Matt drove up to the gates, he knew something was wrong. For one thing, Rick was standing there, waving him off.

Matt rolled down his window. "What is it?"

"Get them out of here. We have a situation."

"What?"

"Leonard Adderson ignored our refusal and showed up with a dozen people wanting cabins."

"Can you handle it?"

"It's being handled right now."

Lorie's concerned voice broke in. "You think he's behind my troubles, don't you?"

Matt glanced her way, galvanized by the fear in her eyes.

"Doesn't matter what I think at this point. I have to keep you safe."

Rick nodded. "Get them out of here. I'll call you when it's all clear."

Matt responded by driving back onto the highway.

"And here I was looking forward to another one of your sister-in-law's really good lunches. I mean, dinners." Lorie's grin looked forced.

"Well, there will be more of those, God willing. In the meantime, what do you all want to eat, and how far are you willing to drive to get it?"

"Anything will be all right." As usual, Margaret sounded as though she didn't want to put him to any extra trouble.

"If you all aren't starving, then let's go a good distance from the Ranch. The farther the better. If we're not there, our perp shouldn't be able to find us."

"I pray not." Lorie rubbed her arms and then turned to look out the window.

They drove through Sister Mountain and, at Crossroads, turned east toward the county line. Matt kept a wary eye on the rearview mirror. If anyone was following them, they were doing such a good job that his superior skills couldn't detect it.

They entered Sidney in neighboring Lanier County, and Matt drove to a little down-home café. It was a charming place, owned by the same family for three generations, and served nothing but old family recipes, aside from a few healthier options they'd added in the past few years. The decor was early 1900s ice-cream-parlor chic. Framed photos decorated the walls, and beside the counter, a blackboard had the day's special scribbled on it in colored chalks.

The Cardinal Café was packed, which was exactly what Matt had hoped for. They were less likely to be noticed in a crowd.

They took seats in the first available booth. By chance or grace, it happened to be positioned where they could keep an eye on the door. Matt made certain he could see his car through the window, so he'd notice if anyone tried to sneak up on it and sabotage it.

"So how long have you been working for the sheriff's department?" Ben asked.

"Since I got back from a tour of duty overseas. I'm still with the reserves, but I probably won't get called back anytime soon. At least I hope not. I enjoy working here at home."

"Is it very challenging?" Margaret asked.

"Most of the time, it's everyday, routine stuff. Traffic stops. Cats up trees. People complaining about noisy neighbors."

"What about the rest of the time?" Lorie asked.

Matt suppressed a grin. "Well, sometimes we get librarians with mysterious notes and exploding cars, but that's the exception rather than the rule."

Lorie chuckled, and, despite the doubts the sheriff had raised, Matt was glad to hear the sound. She had a musical laugh. It made him long to hear it more often. Say, every day for the rest of his life. Unless she ended up in the federal pen for drug trafficking...

"What was your last case before you got my call? If you can tell me, that is."

The waitress arrived with menus, and they took a moment to order what looked good. After she sashayed off, Matt resumed the conversation.

"It was a meth-lab investigation. Someone has to have alerted them, or they wouldn't have been able to pull up stakes and disappear like that. We'll get them eventually, though. We just need better intelligence reports."

"We'll pray you're able to round them up soon." Margaret gave him a smile. Matt could see where Lorie got her beauty.

The conversation turned to more pleasant things. The waitress brought their order, after which they blessed the food and started eating.

Lorie's cell phone rang.

Lorie checked the display, then looked at Matt. "I don't know who this is."

Matt held out his hand. Lorie put the phone into it.

Matt flipped it open and hit the answer button, putting it on speaker.

"You have been a very naughty girl, haven't you, going to the law like that. Shame on you." The robot-processed voice was back.

Lorie turned pale. Margaret grabbed Ben's arm. Matt put a finger to his lips.

"But then you know that, don't you? I'm surprised at you, trusting a deputy. When he finds out the truth, you'll finally be accountable."

Combined with the call Gerhardt had fielded, all Matt's dark suspicions came flooding back. *Was* she responsible for more than justifiable homicide? Lorie's expression held no hint of guilt, just confusion and fear.

"Why are you tormenting me?" Lorie demanded. "What did I ever do to you?"

"Why, you killed Grayson, of course. You have to be punished for that, since the court let you go."

"But I was innocent."

"You shot him. He died. End of story."

"Are you family of his, or what? I didn't mean to kill

him. I was only trying to stop him from killing Ms. Montoya and me."

"I know what happened, and I know what you say happened. Those two things don't jibe. You wanted out of the operation and he wasn't about to let you go. You killed him and then made the courts believe it was self-defense."

Lorie turned very white, and then very red. She looked angry.

"Now wait just a minute here. I don't know what you think I am, but I was never involved in any sort of operation. I had no call or reason to want Grayson Carl dead. A lot of other people may have wanted him dead, but I wasn't in that number. Got it?"

"You talk a good game, Ms. Narramore, but it's coming to an end. You'll finally get what you deserve. I hope your life insurance is up to date."

A cold rage settled in Matt's stomach.

Click.

Dial tone.

Matt looked at Lorie. She still looked furious, or frightened. Probably both. Tears trickled down her mother's face. Despite his doubts, Matt wanted to gather them up and hide them in a cave until the vicious psychopath on the other end of the line was either dead or in custody. He wanted to keep them all safe, but he wasn't sure how much longer he could.

Lorie wondered how she'd manage to eat even a bite of the delicious-looking chicken salad in front of her. The phone call had destroyed her appetite.

"I'm not hungry anymore."

"Eat anyway. You need to keep up your strength." Matt patted her hand. Lorie wished she could throw herself in his arms and hold on for dear life, but even if she believed it to be a good idea, in the middle of a crowded café during the lunch rush was hardly the ideal moment. Especially not with her parents in the audience.

Lorie picked up a fork and pierced a bite of salad. It smelled so good. Why wasn't she hungry? Aside from the obvious reason that someone was out to kill her and her parents because she had been found not guilty of murder.

"Try to eat, honey." Mom sounded so like how she had when Lorie had been little and not feeling well.

Lorie forced the bite into her mouth and chewed. It tasted like sawdust. She swallowed it anyway and took a long drink of the sweet tea. The liquid reached her taste buds where the chicken had failed. She took another long draft of it.

Mom and Dad started eating as well, paying plenty of attention to their plates, although Mom kept glancing in her direction. Matt kept a surreptitious eye alternating between the door and the window overlooking the car. Lorie guessed he was watching to make certain nobody tampered with it. After what had happened to her car while she was in the library, keeping watch was a good idea.

Driven. That's what the perp seemed to be. Driven to destroy her, and for reasons that seemed to be based on speculation and delusion. There was nothing she could do to reason with him—no way to convince him she didn't deserve to die. All she could do was hope and pray that he'd be caught before she or her family were harmed.

The next bite of chicken salad tasted more like chicken salad. The bite after that was actually good.

"Hmm. Not bad."

Matt smiled at her. "Sawdust syndrome?"

"Huh?"

"Shock, grief…things like that can make food taste like sawdust. Or worse."

"How'd you know?"

Matt grinned. "Been there. Choked on that."

His comment made Lorie smile in spite of herself. "How do you do it?"

"What, my job?"

Lorie nodded as she ate more of the salad.

"I can't say it's easy, but it's my chosen career. Plus I love solving problems for people. I think if I hadn't become a law-enforcement officer, I'd have considered becoming a private detective."

The rest of the salad went down fairly easily, and the waitress came and replenished their tea at intervals. Bottomless glasses of sweet tea apparently were part of the tradition of the Cardinal Café. Lorie decided if she lived through this, she'd like to come back sometime when she wasn't under such stress.

Maybe with Matt.

On a date?

No, she wouldn't think about that. Not now. Maybe not ever.

They finished their first course, and the waitress suggested dessert, letting them know that the gingerbread was especially fine today, and that there were hot apple turnovers fresh out of the oven.

They took a split order. Mom and Lorie had the gingerbread, and the men took the hot apple turnovers.

As they lingered over dessert, Matt's phone rang.

He hauled it out of his pocket and stuck it to his ear. "MacGregor." He was silent for a moment. "Oh, good. Thanks, Jim." Another brief silence, when Jim's voice could not be heard over the clatter of flatware and clinking of glasses from the crowded café.

"Right. We'll head back then. Be sure you don't stop watching. Lorie had another call from that maniac while we were here in the restaurant." Another pause. "You're right. I didn't think of that. We'll do something about that right now. Thanks. Yes. See you soon."

Matt switched off the phone and stuck it back in his

pocket. "Jim thinks maybe they're tracking you through the GPS device in your phone."

Lorie turned pale.

"You mean, my phone is bugged?"

"Not bugged. On the grid. Most newer phones have a tracking device in them so the phone companies are able to track their customers, where they are, how much they're calling."

"But they shouldn't give that information out to people."

"They don't, but a good hacker can break into the system and find phones that way."

"What can I do?"

"I have an idea."

Matt's idea was to remove the battery, effectively killing its GPS.

"I don't know what I'll do without my phone."

"We'll get you a burner phone with prepaid minutes."

"But what if he wants to call me and keeps getting routed to voice mail? Won't that make him angry?"

Matt's expression was grave. "He's angry already. This will simply make it harder for him to find you."

If he hasn't already... The thought hung unspoken in the air between them.

"What about Mom's and Dad's phones?"

"Let's leave it at yours for now, until we know more."

"Fine."

They carried out the plan, stopping to buy a cheap phone with about fifty dollars' worth of time on it.

Lorie couldn't help wondering whether they were doing the right thing, removing their line of communication with the stalker. On the one hand, it took away the chance of his tracking her by her phone. On the other hand, it lost them any chance of being able to trace him in turn, or trick him into revealing his plans. After all, if she hadn't gotten the phone call from him earlier, she wouldn't have even realized her parents were in danger. What other crucial information might she miss? Only time would tell, and time was running out.

FIFTEEN

Matt headed back toward the ranch the long way around, taking the scenic route through Lanier County. Despite gathering clouds, the pines and oaks lining the winding mountain road made Matt feel a million miles from danger. It took conscious effort not to let down his guard.

"I always forget how beautiful Lanier County is." Margaret sighed from the backseat. "How come we don't drive over here more often, Ben?"

"We get busy in our little rut, I guess, sweetheart."

Sweetheart. Matt had noticed that Ben frequently called his wife *honey* and *sweetheart*. Matt had always considered endearments annoying. Now the words sounded charming. Would Lorie like being called *sweetheart*, he wondered, or would she prefer something more like *sweetie* or *sugar*, or *sweet face*? She did have a very sweet face. It matched her personality. He'd thought that, after Lorene, maybe he'd never find a woman he could love for the rest of his life. Of course, he wasn't sure Lorie filled that bill, but he'd had an unrealistic list of characteristics he'd expected in his future wife.

If the list he recalled was accurate, he'd wanted a good housekeeper who was beautiful, wanted half a dozen children—three of each gender—and someone who could cook and loved the Lord. Not only would she not mind his hunting and fishing every now and again but she'd also know how to dress a deer as well as gut and scale fish.

Since meeting Lorie, however his ideals had begun to change. He couldn't picture her field dressing a deer, but he could see her with children clustered around her as she read to them, probably using all kinds of interesting voices. He pictured her walking hand in hand with him through the meadow, picking wildflowers. He could even see her up on horseback, riding along beside him, a Stetson on her head and new Justin Boots on her feet, with denim Wranglers and a snap-front shirt in between.

In short, his new ideal was beginning to look more and more like Lorie Narramore. But was he allowing dreams to take the place of reality again? He'd had his future with Lorene all planned out in his head, never realizing how it was all falling apart in front of him. What secrets or surprises was Lorie keeping from him? Was she really guilty, as her stalker claimed?

In this conflicted state of mind, as they rounded a sloping curve on Chastain Mountain, he wasn't prepared for Lorie's scream.

"Look out!"

The oversize black Ram pickup truck struck the side of their car. Matt fought for control of the steering wheel.

A second sideswipe sent them flying off the road. Losing control of the brakes and steering, they careened down the mountainside, the car tumbling like a rockslide, bouncing and flipping before it came to rest, wedged between several pine trees.

Matt blacked out.

Lorie awoke in pain. Oh, she had a really *bad* headache. She could taste blood. And she felt dizzy, like she was standing on her head or something. She heard a whimpering noise behind her.

"It's okay." Dad's voice sounded shaky. "It's okay, Meg, my love. We're alive."

"But what about Lorie?"

Lorie tried to speak, but her voice came out in a hoarse whisper. Clearing her throat, she tried again. "I think I'm alive. What happened?"

"A truck ran us off the road." Dad sounded as though he were moving around.

Lorie took stock of her surroundings. She almost *was* upside down. More like three-quarters of the way flipped over, and part of her was crushing Matt.

"Matt. Matt, are you okay? Can you hear me?"

Matt groaned, and it was a beautiful sound. He was alive.

"Wake up, Matt. Are you hurt?"

"Anybody get the number of the locomotive that hit us?"

Lorie sighed with relief. He must be all right. His sense of humor was intact.

"We've got to get out of here."

"Where's here?"

"I think we landed in some trees."

"Do you have one of those safety escape devices to cut the seat belts, maybe break open a window?" Dad asked.

"In the front pocket. Can you reach it, Lorie? I'd try, but you're blocking my arm."

Lorie felt like she'd pass out any minute, from being suspended from the seat belt and harness. "I'll see."

She reached for the pocket, aware that opening it could dump all the contents on her and scatter them out of reach. But she had to do it, and soon. If all those shows on TV were right, the damage the car had taken in the fall meant the gas tank could explode. At the very least, the people who'd driven them off the road might arrive to make sure they were dead.

Help me, Lord.

The car pocket was jammed. Lorie pushed the button again and again to gain access, but it wasn't budging.

"It won't open."

"Probably the angle. Try pushing and holding it down."

Hard. It was too hard. But Lorie could smell gasoline leaking—if the gas tank had been damaged then they were in serious trouble. It might burst into flames at any moment. Especially if the people who'd run them off the road came down and tossed a match. They wouldn't even have to shoot them. They could burn them alive and be done with it. Everyone would think it was an accident.

Lorie shivered. *Please Lord, help me open the pocket and get the escape device. I can't do it on my own.*

Lorie pressed the button again, and tried sticking her thumbnail in the seam where the door fastened. Maybe she could pry it open.

The door wiggled a tiny bit.

"It's moving, I think…"

Lorie tried the maneuver again.

Her thumbnail broke.

"Ouch."

"Are you hurt?" Mom's voice sounded as though she were fighting panic.

"No, just broke a nail. I'll be fine as soon as we get out of here."

Her thumbnail had been stronger than her fingernails. Lorie wished she had superstrong nails, or at least acrylic nails, instead of the short length she kept for work and for playing the piano.

Lord…

"If I could only reach my purse." She struggled, making the attempt, but hanging upside down, it was impossible. "Everybody pray with me that it'll open this time. If we all agree in faith…"

"Lord, we ask You to help Lorie get that pocket open, in Jesus's name." Dad spoke up quickly, before Matt could.

Matt moaned again.

Lorie didn't think the sound was so beautiful now, because he sounded as though he were in serious pain. He needed a doctor. They probably all did.

"Okay. Here goes. One. Two. THREE."

Lorie gave a tremendous push and pulled on the seam with all her might. It gave, and the contents spilled past her overturned lap.

"Ouch." The tool they needed hit Lorie's neck, slicing a hole in it.

"Are you okay?"

"Yes, Mom." *I'll fix me later.*

She took the device off her throat and slipped the blade onto her seat belt harness.

"Don't fall on your head, baby."

"She won't," Matt assured her. "She'll fall on me."

"Oh, dear."

Lorie pushed the cutter across the webbing. It was sturdy, and didn't want to give way to the blade. Lorie sawed at it.

This will work. Lord, please let this work.

When the webbing was nearly sliced through, it gave way, and Lorie fell onto Matt's shoulder. He made a stifled *mpfh* sound.

"I didn't hurt you, did I?"

"I'm fine. Just get me out of here, and then we'll get your parents free."

Lorie turned in the close quarters. Her face hovered above his.

"Oh, you *are* hurt." Blood trickled from a cut in his forehead. He must have hit his head on the steering wheel. The lack of frontal impact kept the air bag from deploying, so there had been no cushioning at all for the blow.

"Never mind that now. We'll get medical help later. First, we have to get out of here. Can you cut me loose?"

Lorie tried to nod, but in their upside-down situation, it was impossible. "I *will* cut you loose, with God's help."

She started sawing on Matt's seat belt. That close to him, she could see little speckles of green in his blue eyes. She hadn't noticed those before. Well, she'd never been this close to him before, aside from the time when she'd cried all over him, and then her eyes had been unfocused with tears.

Help, Lord. Now is not the time.

She freed him more quickly than she'd been able to cut herself loose, since she was no longer hampered by the friction against her belt. And the closer she came to releasing him, the more a single, ridiculous thought ran through her mind.

Hold me.

But she couldn't say that. Even though it was all she wanted. To get out of this car, rescue Mom and Dad, and then have Matt wrap his arms around her and never let go. Maybe throw in a few kisses for good measure.

But this was neither the time nor the place for that sort of nonsense. Even after they escaped from the car, their situation would still be dangerous. They were injured, without transport, miles from anywhere with no one sure of their exact location except for the maniac who had driven them off the road.

Matt snapped the rest of the webbing before Lorie finished cutting.

"Now, break open that window. You'll have to crawl out first."

Lorie shook her head. "I don't want to rain glass on you."

"Don't worry about that. I'll hold you up."

Matt's strong hands pushed Lorie's back up into a position where she could get a whack at the window. The glass only cracked when she first hit it.

"Hit it really hard. Give it all you've got. We'll close our eyes. Cover your eyes back there if you can."

"Got it," Dad said.

"Mine are covered, too," Mom piped in.

"All right. Hit it again, and this time pretend it's the person who's been tormenting you and threatening your parents."

Lorie pulled back and whacked the window, picturing a nameless villain standing there. "Take that, you coward!" The window shattered, raining glass pebbles on them.

Able at last to reach her purse, she slung the strap over her arm. Lorie reached outside the window, cutting her hand on something sharp, and tried to pull herself through. Soon she'd be free at last. But what if they couldn't get her parents out? What then?

Matt gave Lorie a boost out through the window.

"She's out."

"Oh, thank the Lord!" Margaret exclaimed.

"We'll get you out of here in just a minute."

Matt reached up to grab the door frame. Lorie was still on the door.

"Jump down. I need to get up there."

"I can't."

"Yes, you can. I have confidence you can do anything you set your mind to. So, set your mind to getting down from there, so I can get out of the car and rescue your parents."

Matt hoped he didn't sound too harsh. He'd apologize later, after they were out of this fix.

The car rocked, and Matt heard Lorie squeak, immediately followed by a rustling crash. A rush of concern constricted his chest.

"You okay?"

"I'll be fine. Let's get Mom and Dad out of there."

Matt looked back at Ben and Margaret. "We'll have you two out of here in a jiffy."

"*Jiffy* doesn't matter, as long as *out of here* is fairly quick."

Matt smiled. As his ranching ancestors might have said, Ben had sand.

Matt pulled himself up through the window and bit his lip. He hadn't realized in what a precarious situation the car was. If the trees hadn't stopped their descent, they'd have fallen all the way down the side of Chastain Mountain into Lanier Creek.

Thank You, Lord. Even in this, Your hand was upon us.

The entire back end of the car had caved in. That Lorie's parents hadn't been crushed showed that God was taking care of them.

But as grateful as he was for the trees, they weren't exactly designed to hold a three-thousand-pound car in place. If they jostled things too much getting Ben and Margaret out, the car could go into free fall again.

Of course, based on the way it was swaying, that might happen no matter what they did.

Matt looked around for Lorie.

"Down here."

Lorie had fallen farther down the side of the mountain, and was resting against the trunk of a black walnut tree. Pine tar covered her hands and a good deal of her Sunday dress.

"You all right?"

"I think so."

The car wobbled again.

Don't let it fall just yet, Lord. Help us to get Ben and Margaret out of there.

Matt extricated himself from the car window, pulling himself out and moving slowly as he could off the car. He pulled the emergency device out of his pocket.

"Cover your eyes again," he instructed the Narramores. "I'm going to smash your window."

Ben and Margaret obeyed. Matt gave the window a mighty blow that shattered it instantly.

Margaret hung almost on top of Ben, the way Lorie had been on him. Matt grasped Margaret's hand so she wouldn't fully drop onto her husband when she was freed, then cut the seat belt with his other hand. Margaret's hand in his was warm and steady, and her grip was firm. He saw what Lorie meant. Her parents *were* tough. His admiration for her and for them rose another notch.

Matt stuck the emergency device back in his pocket and grabbed Margaret's other hand. "Ben, if you can push while I pull… We need to get Margaret out of here without hurting her."

"Gotcha."

The maneuver was tricky, but with Ben's help, Margaret came through the lower window much more easily than Lorie had, even with a purse twice the size of her daughter's.

"Oh, my goodness." Margaret's eyes grew wide as she took in their situation. "We're halfway down the mountain."

"Grab hold of that branch and don't let go. I've got to get Ben out of there."

Margaret nodded.

Matt heard her checking on Lorie, but he concentrated on Lorie's father as he lowered himself halfway through the smashed window to reach Ben's seat belt.

"That truck had California plates."

"Oh?"

"I got a good look at it."

Matt sawed at Ben's seat belt. "Don't suppose you… got a number?"

"AC something, and I think the last number was 9. It

was an older-model truck too. That would fit in with the plate."

"Truck fan?"

"Anything with wheels." Ben grinned. He took a deep breath and moaned. "I think I've got some broken ribs. Don't tell the girls."

"That's going to make it harder to extricate you without injuring you."

"Just get me out of here, and then we'll worry about my injuries."

"We don't want to puncture a lung."

"Then pray we don't."

Matt nodded. "Okay. Seat belt is sawed through, as you probably noticed."

"I'm ready."

"Let me crawl back out of here, and then I'll help you through."

Ben nodded. "Go for it."

Matt inched backward through the smashed window, feeling glass score his stomach. He'd worry about that later.

The car wobbled again.

Lord, don't let it go. Hold us up a little longer.

"This thing going to be stable enough for me to get out?"

"Yup." He spoke with a lot more confidence than he felt. "God's holding it. You grab my hands."

Ben's grip was a lot firmer than Matt had expected. Lorie's dad must work out. Good. That was one less concern. The Lord knew they had enough on their collective plate right now.

The effort to pull himself up like that clearly cost Ben a great deal, and he moaned despite trying to remain quiet. Matt knew he was endeavoring to keep "his girls" from worrying.

It was hard enough to remember to cast every care on

the Lord when things were going well. But a situation like this was impossible without the Lord's help.

Lord, I'm casting every care on You, starting right now. Help me remember You care for me, and for Lorie and Margaret and Ben, too.

Branches cracked and groaned as Matt gave a mighty pull. Ben popped out the car window like a cork from a bottle.

All the extra motion was too much stress on the pines that had caught them. The car shook as branches cracked, sounding like an earthquake. A split second later, car and branches fell free down the side of the mountain.

With crashes that echoed across the valley below, it plunged to the bottom. The ghost of a splash reached their ears.

"Are you okay? Ben?"

"I'm alive, Margaret."

Matt noticed Ben didn't say he was okay. Ben wasn't all right. None of them were, not completely. Matt had to find a way to get them out of here, up the side of the mountain and back onto the road. Assuming the truck that had run them off in the first place had gone… But either way, they needed help as soon as they could get it.

Matt reached into his other pocket for his cell phone. Pulling it out, the screen shattered in his hand. He tried to turn it on anyway, with predictable results.

Great. They were injured and stranded out in the middle of nowhere on the side of a mountain without cell phone reception.

"Try your phone," Matt said to Ben. "See if you can get a signal. Mine's broken."

Ben reached into his pocket, with effort, as he sat on the prickly pine needles. Extricating it, he flipped it open. He met Matt's eyes.

"No bars."

Margaret tried hers, and shook her head.

Lorie's phone was their last hope.

"Check that new phone of yours, will you, Lorie?"

She pulled it from her purse and held it for everyone to see. "We haven't charged the battery yet. How about if I try my old phone?"

Margaret and Ben exchanged a nervous glance.

Matt nodded. "See if you can get a signal."

Lorie snapped the battery back into her old phone and turned it on, fear mingling with hope on her face. A moment later, hope faded. She shook her head and disconnected the battery again.

Matt sighed as she replaced it in the purse.

"Okay. Here's the deal. We're going to have to try to climb out of here, either up or down. Believe it or not, I think up would be better. It would be too easy to slip going downhill."

Lorie looked at her parents, then at Matt.

"Not to worry about us, kiddo." Ben was putting on a brave face. "Your mother and I aren't ready to check out yet."

"I know you guys love to go hiking, but this isn't exactly a stroll through Balboa Park."

"We're in good shape, sweetie. Don't worry about us." Margaret clearly was trying to be brave, too. Maybe she'd fool her daughter, but Matt didn't think so. After the crash, none of them was in any condition to climb out of here. Yet they had no choice but to try.

Lorie opened her purse and removed a small first-aid kit. "This isn't much, but hold still." She squirted some antibiotic cream onto Matt's forehead, unwrapped a bandage and pressed it on top of the wound. Her gentle touch only reminded him of their uncertain situation.

"Thanks." He'd have said more, but words stuck in his throat.

Fear gripped Matt in ways he hadn't experienced since coming home from Afghanistan. Three people now depended on him to get them out of the woods and back to civilization—without the bad guys finding them first.

SIXTEEN

Lorie tried to assess their situation calmly, but this reminded her too much of scary movies she'd seen that started with people being lost and hurt in the forest. Dad hadn't said anything, but he was moving a little too carefully. His face was drawn with pain. *He must be badly injured.*

She looked at her mother, who appeared more determined than frightened. Mom must have noticed about Dad but had apparently decided not to let him know she realized he was injured. Well, if Mom could be that brave, Lorie could, too.

Lorie looked up at the side of the mountain, unable to spot the point from which they'd fallen. It was so far that she couldn't see the road at all. The car must have tumbled several hundred yards almost straight down.

Thank You that we're not worse off, Lord. Please keep us safe.

Because the danger was nowhere near over.

She hoped Matt still had his sidearm. And she hoped he had a lot of bullets. She prayed he wouldn't need to use them.

Matt picked up a broken branch about four feet long. "Anybody need a hiking stick?"

"I'll take it." Ben spoke quietly. "That is, if no one else needs it." He looked at his wife and daughter.

Mom shook her head.

"You take it, Dad."

He accepted it then, and leaned on it, looking grateful.

Lorie studied Matt's face. He was worrying. By his expression, he didn't want them to know.

Lorie's leg ached.

Lord, You're going to have to hike through me.

Mom spoke up. "Before we start, let's pray."

Lorie looked at her mom. "Good idea. You want to start?"

Mom nodded and held out her hands. They formed a little circle.

"Lord, we thank You for delivering us out of the hand of our enemies. We ask You now to guide us out of the wilderness to safety. We agree on this in Jesus's name."

Dad took up the prayer. "Lord, thank You for Your protection and Your love."

Matt spoke next. "Lord, thank You for Lorie and Margaret and Ben and for bringing us all together, although I wish it had been under different circumstances. I don't understand what Your will is in this, but I trust You. Don't let us make a wrong step, Lord. Thanks."

Matt squeezed Lorie's hand.

"Father, I lift my heart to You. You've been so gracious to me through everything. I'm sorry I didn't react better. Thank You for being here with us. Amen."

Everyone else echoed her amen. Lorie felt a burden lift. It was going to be all right.

They started walking, slowly, haltingly. Ben had to stop every few feet to draw a worryingly ragged breath.

At first, Matt led the way, but then he stopped.

"Lorie, you take the lead. I'm going to bring up the rear, in case your dad needs help."

"I'm okay," Ben protested.

"It's better if Lorie goes first. I can keep a weather eye out in both directions this way."

Lorie nodded.

"Keep on a slight climb." Matt bent and picked up another stick. "Here. Use this for balance on the downhill side. I don't want you sliding down the mountain."

"What about you and Mom?"

Matt looked around. "There's bound to be more sticks in the vicinity. We'll pick them up as we find them. In the meantime, your mom can lean on me."

"Thank you." Mom gave him a smile and then they were back on their way.

Lorie headed out slowly, picking her way cautiously around odd rock outcroppings and loose scree.

"Careful here." She looked at the rock field. "I wish we didn't have to cross it." She looked up the hill. It was almost perpendicular in spots. She glanced down at her flimsy sandals. Not a good combination.

"I wish we had some rope," Dad said with a sigh. "We could tie ourselves together."

"Why don't you wish for some pitons and crampons while you're at it, Ben?" Instead of sounding sarcastic, Mom's voice was full of affection.

Lorie smiled. "I wish we had a compass and map."

"How about a helicopter?" Matt suggested.

"I don't like to fly," Mom said, and then laughed. Her laughter scared away a pair of cardinals.

"One good thing."

They all looked at Matt expectantly.

"When my family realizes we aren't on our way back and that they can't reach me by phone, they'll call out the troops."

"Then we better pray they'll start trying to reach you soon."

Matt nodded.

The problem was, it might be a while before they could try to reach them. Would the situation with Adderson at Rob Roy Ranch be cleared up before nightfall?

* * *

They could only travel at a crawl, but the sun seemed to have sped up. At this rate, it would be dark soon. They'd get hungry before then, and Matt hadn't spotted any convenient berries growing on bushes yet.

Matt lost track of how long they'd walked. Periodically he checked his watch, but time tended to lose meaning in situations like these.

When the sun progressed farther west, it sank behind the crest of the mountain. Not good. The shadows would cool things down in a hurry.

"Lorie."

She stopped and looked back at him.

"We need to stop and see about shelter for the night."

"Where?"

"Here, or somewhere fairly close." He peered through the trees. "Over there. It looks like it evens up a bit. We'll make camp there."

Lorie nodded. "All right. I don't think any of us is good for much longer."

"Have you ever camped out in the woods before?"

"Not without a camping trailer." Ben grinned. "Margaret does like her creature comforts."

"Right now, a place to lie down, hopefully free of bugs, seems like a dream come true." His wife smiled and patted his arm. "It feels as though we've been walking forever."

"Or at least three weeks." Lorie smiled, then turned back to Matt. "Do you want to go ahead to check it out?"

"No. We should stick together. We'll just have to keep moving till we get there. If it isn't suitable, we'll find a way to make do."

The ground leveled out in a small outcropping of rock. Earth had puddled in the area for centuries, making a small meadow on the side of the mountain with grass still short enough that it would be comfortable for sleeping.

"What about making a fire?" Lorie asked.

"You're reading my mind." Matt's smile was encouraging as he helped Margaret and Ben to sit on the ground.

"Maybe we can get a cell-phone signal from here." Ben dug out his phone and opened it. "Very faint. One bar, and it comes and goes."

"Give it a shot. Call 911."

Ben punched the numbers and the send button.

The air was still enough for Matt to be able to hear the operator's voice on the other end. "Nine-one-one. What is the nature of your emergency?"

"We've been run off the road on Highway 32 just south of Trueheart. There are four of us, and we're injured."

"—signal breaking up. Can you repeat your lo—"

"Cell-phone reception is really bad here. We're injured. Halfway down the mountain from Highway 32 south of Trueheart. Please send help."

"Stay on the line. We'll—"

The phone line went dead.

Ben looked at Matt, desperation in his eyes. "It went. We lost the signal."

"You tried. And the message might have gotten through."

Lorie tapped Matt's arm. "Let's find some firewood."

"We'll need to clear away the grass for about three feet in a circle and dig a ways."

"With sticks?"

"Unless you have a handy-dandy shovel tucked away in your pocket that I don't know about."

"I don't." Lorie thought a moment, then smiled. "But I do have a knife in my purse."

"Good. That'll also help us get the fire started. Get a rock. Flint if you can find it. Oil shale should work, too. I'll dig. You gather up some twigs and fallen branches. Dry ones."

"Boy Scout?"

It was Matt's turn to smile. "Boy Scout wannabe and survival training in the air force."

Lorie turned to carry out his orders. Good. She wasn't going to question his authority. That was vital. In a survival situation, somebody had to be the leader, preferably the one who knew what to do.

Despite the phone call to 911, Matt knew the odds of their survival would greatly increase if they stayed in one spot, all together, and made a fire. Four people in a group were easier to find than individuals scattered around the woods. Of course, that could be a problem, too. Even if they were found…as easily as the fire could alert rescuers, it could draw their enemies.

Lorie had crossed plenty of rocks on her way to the clearing, but the little meadow didn't seem to have many of its own. Twigs, either.

Lorie glanced up at the sky. There should still be enough daylight left, she hoped, for her to find what they needed. Of course, they really needed water and food, but next to that, warmth would be vital if they weren't found before nightfall.

She picked up a few rocks that looked as though they might strike a spark on steel. She didn't want to test them herself for fear of setting off an unintended fire. No sense adding arson to her record.

At the edge of the little meadow, plenty of fallen branches, last year's pinecones and needles littered the undergrowth. Lorie gathered as much as she could, making a carrying pouch of her skirt.

Matt had made a good start on clearing the ground. He'd made a hole, and was ripping the turf off with his bare hands.

"Would my knife help?"

Matt looked up at her and smiled. "Only if it isn't one of those little dainty penknives with a nail file and—"

Lorie threw a pinecone at him.

Matt caught it. "Hey! What's that for?"

"Insulting my knife." Lorie dumped her load of cones, rocks and branches and stooped to dig around in her purse. "These rocks look okay?"

Matt chose one. "This will do. Let's see that knife."

Lorie pulled out a folding knife with a lock blade.

"Whoa. I thought you'd be a Swiss Army knife kind of girl."

"I make things for the library crafts program. This is my carving knife."

Matt got a new look of respect in his eyes. "Okay if I cut turf with it?"

"Be my guest. I can hone it again later." Lorie put it into his hand.

"Thanks." Matt opened the knife and studied the blade with approval. "Nice and sharp."

"Dull knives are dangerous. I'll be back." Lorie turned to head back to the edge of the clearing. "Are these twigs okay for starters?"

"Perfect. Pinecones, too. See if you can find some bigger branches. I'll help you when I get the ground clear."

Lorie nodded. Stopping to check on Mom and Dad, who sat at the edge of where Matt was working, her fears rose again. Dad's normally rosy complexion had turned a pasty gray. Lorie reached out a finger and took his pulse. Although it was steady, it seemed a little too fast for someone who'd been sitting for the past twenty minutes.

"You okay, Dad?"

Dad nodded. "I'll be fine, cupcake. Just hurry up with the wood, okay?"

Mom glanced at her, a world of things in her eyes that Lorie knew she wouldn't say. Mom would never deliberately worry Dad.

"I'll hurry. You both stay warm."

Lorie spotted a bunch of fallen branches near the edge of the woods.

The branches felt dry to the touch. *Thank You, Lord.*

Lorie had tried starting a fire with damp branches before, without much success. Pity there wasn't a nice pile of chopped wood around here. Of course, that would mean someone nearby, which could also be a good thing. Or a bad thing, if it wasn't a good person.

Now that she'd thought about it, Lorie remembered Matt had been hunting a meth lab. It reminded her to be careful. Not everybody in the backwoods was there for the peace and quiet.

Lord, thank You for rescuing us. I know You'll keep us safe.

Lorie carried an armload of sticks when she returned to the clearing. Dad was shivering, even though the temperatures hadn't dropped much. Lorie was thankful it was not still early spring. Mom had draped both arms around Dad's shoulders.

Lorie dropped the sticks beside Matt and went straight over to her dad. She laid a hand on his forehead. It was much too hot. Running a fever couldn't be good. She wondered whether he'd broken anything in the crash.

"Dad, are you all right?"

"I will be, cupcake."

Mom's eyes said otherwise, but she didn't utter a word.

What was there to say? There was nothing they could do to make themselves any safer, any healthier, or any more protected from the dangers of the wilderness. And from the other dangers that had landed them there. Lorie watched Matt coax the fire into life and stayed silent, as well.

SEVENTEEN

Matt looked at Lorie over their small fire. "You get some rest. I'll take the first watch."

"I don't think I can sleep."

"Try anyway. You, too, Margaret, Ben. This was a huge strain on your systems."

"All right. I'll try."

Margaret lay down beside Ben, and Lorie curled up next to her and closed her eyes.

Lorie wasn't aware she was asleep until she felt someone shaking her shoulder.

"Lorie." Matt's voice, low and urgent, called her.

"Mmm."

"I can't stay awake any longer. Can you man the fire?"

Lorie blinked and rubbed her eyes. Disorientation gave way to awareness. The wreck. The clearing. The fire. They were in the woods, waiting for a rescue that might never come.

Lorie sat up, taking care not to disturb Mom.

"Okay. I'm awake. Have a nice nap."

"Thanks. I fed the fire just now."

Lorie looked at the pile of firewood they'd collected. It was a lot smaller than she remembered. Matt must have used a lot of wood.

"Do you think it'll last the night?"

But Matt was already dozing.

Left alone with everyone asleep, Lorie looked up at the stars. The array of constellations told her she must have slept quite a while. They were so bright out here in the mountains, even brighter than at her house in Wolf Hollow. Too many people had those halogen security lights these days, even out in the country. It was never pitch-black dark the way she remembered from her childhood.

"When I consider the firmament, the work of Your hands, what is man, that Thou art mindful of him?"

The psalmist must have been sitting out on the hills on a night like this when he made that song. She wished she knew the tune that went with it. How wonderful would it be to be able to sing the words in its original Hebrew?

Off in the distance, Lorie heard a new import from Texas. A pack of coyotes yipped as the waning moon peeked over the horizon.

Lord, please keep the coyotes away from us.

Of all the ends she could imagine, being eaten by coyotes was not high on her list of favorite ways to die. At least a bullet would be quick.

The fire was getting too low. Lorie added a stick.

The fire sputtered.

Oh, Lord, no. Please don't let it go out.

The flame licked at the new source of fuel. After a minute, it crackled merrily.

Lorie let out a breath of relief, and reminded herself that, aside from the mosquitoes, the smoke and all their injuries, this wasn't too bad. They could be a lot worse off. Well, maybe not a *lot* worse off, but worse off.

Lorie began to whistle softly, barely making any noise. She needed help to stay awake.

There's nothing like knowing you have to be awake to make you sleepy. Remind me not to do this again, Lord. As if it had been her choice in the first place.

The moon rose higher in the sky, dimming the stars.

A noise in the woods brought Lorie to attention. She sat up straighter, glad she hadn't been staring into the fire.

She turned toward the mountain, rising to her feet, picking up the walking stick. It wouldn't make much of a weapon. Not if their pursuer had a gun.

Lord, help.

Lorie peered at the area of wood where the crashing noise had come from. It was so dark in the trees. The moonlight wasn't strong enough to penetrate the thick tangle of branches.

Lorie's stomach clenched. It was out there, whatever "it" was. Was it her pursuer? The person who had threatened everything she held dear?

A head emerged out of the trees, followed by a body supported by four spindly legs.

A deer.

Lorie giggled. It really was funny. She'd been frightened half out of her wits by Bambi.

Her cry of laughter woke Matt, whose eyes flew open. "Is everything all right?"

Lorie put a finger to her lips.

"It was a deer," she whispered.

Matt sat up. "Pity it isn't hunting season. We could eat it."

Eat Bambi? Lorie tamped down her instinctive horror. For survival, she could probably eat just about anything, but… "I don't think I'm that hungry yet."

"I—" Matt broke off.

"What is it?"

Matt held up his hand for silence.

Lorie froze, listening. Something else behind the deer alerted it, and the deer bounded off into the forest.

Someone was coming.

Matt drew his gun and aimed it at the trees.

In the darkness, a hoarse stage whisper echoed through the woods.

"Murdererrrrr."

Fear stabbed Lorie through the heart. He was *here!*

A flash of red blinded her for a moment. Matt shoved her to the ground as a rifle report echoed across the valley. Sighting on the flash and the laser, Matt fired off three rounds at the shooter.

The noise of someone grunting in pain reached their ears as Mom and Dad wakened.

"What—?" Mom squeaked.

"Stay down!"

"Hey!" A new voice invaded the woods. "Someone's shooting!"

The laser light disappeared as the shooter crashed through the woods.

A bulky figure with a flashlight came through the trees. Apparently he saw Matt's gun, for he froze in his tracks.

Matt spoke into the night. "Stop right there! Don't come any closer."

"Hey, I'm not your shooter! I saw a man with a rifle running away as I arrived. Are you the folks whose car went down the ravine? We've been looking for you."

"And you are?"

"Lanier County Volunteer Fire Search and Rescue. We're the ones the 911 call went through to."

"You got any ID?"

"Sure do."

Margaret and Ben sat up, now that the danger was apparently past, but Matt noticed that Lorie seemed more wary, raising up on one elbow as if she wanted to be ready to flee if necessary. Smart girl.

The man came closer to the fire, holding out an ID card along with the flashlight.

"Sam McGee, Lanier County volunteer coordinator."

"Matt MacGregor, Dainger County Sheriff's Department."

Matt shook his hand, squelching the impulse to grab the man's flashlight and take off after the shooter. He couldn't take that risk. Unlikely as it was, McGee *could* be one of the people after Lorie. Leaving the Narramores alone with anyone was not an option, even if he *was* with Search and Rescue.

"We've got a truck right up the mountain. Who was shooting at you?"

"Wish we knew. We've got some injuries. One man with broken ribs, everyone else with scrapes and contusions. I suppose you didn't get a lead on the truck that ran us off the road."

Sam shook his head. "Sorry. I'm just glad we found you. We were supposed to call off the search at dark, but I couldn't rest." He looked at Ben. "I don't know how we're going to get him up the mountain in the shape he's in."

"I was hoping for a helicopter."

Sam chuckled. "Hope on. We don't have one."

Matt shook his head. "Figured it was a long shot."

Sam took the radio from his belt clip. "W5DOG this is KG5OSB. Found 'em."

The radio crackled. "Roger that, KG5OSB. Woohoo! What do you need, over?"

"Stretcher down to Foster's Meadow, pronto, over."

"Stretcher. Roger. Be there in fifteen."

"And call the sheriff's department. Let them know there's a shooter."

"Will do. W5DOG, over and out."

"KG5OSB out." Sam stuck the Handie-Talkie back on his belt.

Matt looked at Sam. "You armed?"

"Got a flare gun, but that won't be much help against a rifle if your guy comes back."

Matt turned his face to the woods. Maybe the shooter was gone. But the way his skin crawled, he was pretty sure they were still being watched.

"We need to douse the fire."

Sam raised his eyebrows.

Lorie said nothing, but started pulling the flames to pieces with a stick.

Dawn was beginning to peek over the horizon when a sky-blue-clad Lanier County Sheriff's Deputy led two paramedics into the clearing.

"Sorry about your welcome to Lanier County." He introduced himself as Deputy Vincent, and the two paramedics, brothers John and Philip Arnaud.

Matt took a moment to check out the area where their shooter had stood. It didn't take long to spot traces of blood. Briefly, he filled Vincent in on what had happened.

"I was pretty sure I hit him, especially when he ran."

"We'll check the hospital for GSWs. Maybe that'll solve your case."

Matt felt a surge of hope. Could it be that simple? He hoped so. Someone with an unexplained gunshot wound turning up right before they did could be the very lead they needed to wrap up the case and protect Lorie once and for all. But he couldn't get ahead of himself. They had to get to the hospital first.

Ben turned out to be a terrible patient. He kept protesting he didn't need to hitch a ride on a stretcher and he could walk on his own.

Matt reminded him that the ribs were broken and he'd had a hard enough time getting to the meadow with them. He'd better behave and let the volunteers do their job, or Matt would be forced to run him in for resisting a rescue.

"Can't be having that, now, can we?" Margaret grinned.

"No, I guess not. I hate to put anybody to the bother."

Lorie smiled at her dad. "Now you're starting to sound like Mom."

"I should, after thirty-two years of marriage."

"That long?" Matt asked. "When was your anniversary?"

"Actually, it's next week."

The two burly rescuers hefted the stretcher holding Dad once they had him firmly strapped down.

"I feel like a sausage with all these straps."

"You're my sausage," Margaret said, leaning over and giving Ben a kiss before they started climbing the mountain.

Emergency vehicles waited on the side of the mountain. Flashing lights competed with the beauty of the dawn.

It took some time to get them checked out. Finally, they determined nobody else had any broken bones, although Margaret had a sprained arm that, of course, she hadn't mentioned, not wanting anyone to worry.

The EMT who had stayed with the vehicles wrapped an elastic bandage around her arm and put it into a sling.

"Now hold on tight, because we'll drive to the hospital right after the SAR unit, so you can be with your husband."

"Okay."

The ambulance took Margaret away.

Lorie and Matt remained with Deputy Vincent, answering questions.

"Can you describe the vehicle that ran you off the road?"

"It was an older-model black Dodge Ram pickup truck with California license plates. The number started with *A*."

Lorie had only seen part of it, but she described the black truck the best she could. "It had those giant, oversize tires. I'm pretty sure the truck left a streak of paint on the top left side of our car, so maybe you can match it."

Matt nodded. "Good idea."

Deputy Vincent radioed for a county-affiliated wrecking company to extricate the car from the bottom of Chastain Mountain. After a short exchange describing the difficulties the driver would face in retrieving the car, he switched off the radio.

"Come on. I'll give you a lift to town."

* * *

For a brief second, Lorie froze at the sight of the deputy's car. The back door stood open, and she flashed back to that night in Coronado, her hands cuffed behind her, the police officer putting a hand on her head to keep her from giving herself a skull fracture.

Matt's voice murmured in her ear. "You're not under arrest now, Lorie. I'm right here with you."

Lorie flashed him a look of gratitude. Taking the hand he held out to her made the car look much less frightening.

Oh, Lord, thank You for Matt's understanding.

A moment later, she was fastening her seat belt and trying to remain calm.

"Sorry y'all have to ride in the back like criminals."

"Not a problem." Matt spoke for both of them.

Lorie was grateful. She couldn't force a response out of her throat.

"The view's really different from back here," Matt continued in a casual tone. "I'm used to being on the other side of the security wire."

Deputy Vincent laughed. "I hope it doesn't smell too bad back there. The last occupant was more than a little drunk, but he managed not to toss his cookies until we stopped by the bushes at the station."

Lorie grimaced as the word picture conjured up an image she'd rather have skipped. But then, she'd have skipped a lot of things lately if her life could have gone back to normal.

Lorie closed her eyes, trying not to imagine herself in handcuffs again. That had been so horrible. But not as horrible as knowing what she'd done to deserve it. She wondered why anyone would deliberately kill another human being. She hadn't had any choice, but if she could have taken it all back and let him kill her instead, she would have, especially when she was carried off to jail. It was horrible. It was a nightmare from which she couldn't wake up.

"Are you okay, Lorie?"

Not really. This is too much, bringing it all back where I can't get rid of it. But she couldn't tell him that.

"I'll be fine."

The usual platitude. The usual cop-out. Not really a lie, just a looking forward to the future rather than dwelling on what was happening. Coating the pain with another layer of self-defense.

This moment was not too good, either.

The car drive through the mountains in the backseat was nauseating. Despite the car smelling all right, the lack of fresh air made Lorie queasy. But she didn't ask the officer to turn up the air. She didn't want to ask for any favors from law enforcement. Even though she had no cause to feel like a prisoner, riding in the backseat of the patrol car brought back everything she had experienced, with the impenetrable wire mesh and safety glass between her and freedom. It was so bad she wondered if she were still sleeping on the side of the mountain, having a horrible nightmare. Maybe she was. Maybe she'd wake up and still be in the meadow.

Better yet, maybe she'd wake up and be in her own bed at home in Scripps Ranch, and none of this would have happened. It was the idea of going to the Hotel Del Coronado and being among all the rich and famous of San Diego County that did it to her. It was only a nightmare.

Only it wasn't.

It had happened. She had gone to jail temporarily, she'd gone on trial and now someone was determined to make her suffer.

Lord, please help me. I can't take much more of this.

The car rounded a curve and traveled down a slope to a town built on the side of the mountain.

Lorie held on for dear life to Matt's hand, but seemed unaware of it.

Was Lorie having a panic attack? Her breathing was rapid, and the color had left her face. The death grip she had on Matt's hand was another clue. Riding in the back of a patrol car must be bringing back everything that had happened to her in San Diego.

Matt squeezed Lorie's hand. The startled look in those lovely brown eyes revealed his suspicion to be true. She hadn't known she was holding his hand.

"Your dad will be all right."

Lorie seemed to hesitate a moment before nodding. "I've been praying."

"So have I." Matt longed to tell Lorie everything was going to work out, that she didn't have to be afraid of riding in a patrol car, but he wasn't sure how much she'd be comfortable with him saying, considering the officer up front listening. He settled for laying his free hand on top of hers. "We'll be at the hospital soon, and then we should know something."

They'd know Lorie's dad's prognosis. But would the criminal who'd forced them off the road and shot at Lorie be waiting for them?

EIGHTEEN

By the time the patrol car pulled up by the hospital's emergency-room entrance, Lorie was jumping at every siren. Knowing her dad was inside made her rush out of the car the moment Deputy Vincent opened the door, barely remembering to thank him before she rushed through the automatic sliding-glass entry.

A world of beeping medical equipment, crying children and overly bright lights stunned her into immobility for a moment. Spotting triage, Lorie looked over the shoulder of a lady with an apparently broken arm.

"Ben Narramore?"

The beefy male nurse in SpongeBob scrubs at the computer nodded his head at the curtained staging areas. "In three, but his wife's with him. You'll have to wait."

"Thanks."

Lorie searched for a chair near unit three, but most of them were already taken—although no one seemed terribly pleased to be in them. The orange plastic seats might have been salvaged from the late 1960s. They looked miserably uncomfortable. Snagging one at the end of a row, she discovered her assessment was correct.

Once she was seated, Lorie remembered Matt. Where was he? Squirming in the chair, she discovered him close to the emergency entrance, talking with Deputy Vincent. After a moment, Vincent removed his radio from his belt and spoke a few terse words into it. It crackled a response. As he reattached it to his utility belt, he handed Matt a cell phone. Matt must have shown him his broken one.

Whom was Matt calling? As she sat there, feeling like a voyeur, Matt made two phone calls. He gave the phone back to Deputy Vincent, shook his hand and then made eye contact with Lorie.

Wending his way through the assorted patients and their families waiting to be seen, Matt reached Lorie's side. Deputy Vincent remained close to the door, keeping an eye on those present.

"Where's your dad?"

Lorie nodded at unit three.

"Let me fill you in." Matt lowered his voice until she could barely hear him over the background of hospital noise. "Lanier County Sheriff's Department put out an APB on the pickup. They found it this morning, abandoned. It came up on the database as stolen from a theater in Branson yesterday."

Lorie shuddered. "And they drove it all the way down here to…"

"Looks that way." Matt laid a warm hand on Lorie's shoulder.

"No sign—"

Matt shook his head. "Not even a gum wrapper. No blood, either. The shooter must have been in another vehicle. They're doing a test for fingerprints, but they don't have the budget for DNA."

"And if he wore gloves—" Lorie broke off as the curtain to unit three opened. Mom scanned the crowd. "Over here, Mom!"

Mom walked over toward them, moving more slowly than Lorie would have expected. She was limping. Lorie jumped up and helped her to the chair she'd just vacated.

"How's Dad?"

"Two broken ribs, three fractured ribs, but no punctured lung or other internal injuries, praise the Lord!"

"What about you?"

Mom shook her head. "It's only a sprain. I'll be fine."

An alarm rang through the hospital, immediately followed by a voice over the PA system.

"Code Amber. Code Amber. Please evacuate the building in a calm and orderly manner." The message repeated.

All around them in the waiting room, patients, orderlies and nurses began to exit through the emergency room doors.

Lorie grabbed Matt's arm. "What is it?"

"Code Amber means it's a bomb threat."

Mom blanched. "We've got to get your dad out of here."

Deputy Vincent wove through the exiting mass of humanity, radio in hand. "We have units on the way."

A man in a white lab coat wheeled Dad's gurney out of unit three as several nurses and orderlies helped other patients toward the sliding glass doors. Instead of following them, he turned the gurney toward the door to the radiology department.

Separating from the others, Lorie followed after him. "Hey!" she shouted. "Aren't you supposed to be taking him outside?"

"Shortcut."

Lorie didn't know her way around this hospital, but she could see the glass sliding doors that led out to the parking lot. Why was he headed in the opposite direction?

"Stop!"

With a smirking glance over his shoulder, the man took off, wheeling the gurney with practiced ease, steering it and throwing open the automatic door switch.

He was kidnapping Dad! Instinct took over. Lorie sprinted after them.

The door slammed shut in her face before she could follow. She shoved it. It refused to open. Panicked, she turned to find the access pressure panel to open the door. Pressing the wheelchair symbol on the aluminum square finally made the door swing open.

Behind her, Lorie heard racing footsteps and scarcely moved out of the way before Matt and Deputy Vincent flew past her, guns drawn. Heart banging fit to burst from her chest, she gave chase, struggling to keep up.

"Stop!" Matt ordered.

The man glanced over his shoulder. Abandoning the gurney, he dashed for the nearest elevator. Matt and Vincent gave chase, but the doors squeaked closed in their faces. Vincent pointed at the door to the staircase, and they raced through it.

Lorie reached her dad's gurney and stopped it a second before it would have slammed into the abandoned radiology nurses' station. She gasped, trying to get her breath.

"Dad, you okay?"

Dad's eyes were slightly glazed, doubtless from pain medication, but he smiled when he saw Lorie. "That was some wild ride, cupcake."

Lorie deliberately slowed her breathing as she scanned the controls of the gurney. How hard could it be to operate?

"We have to get out of here. There's a bomb threat."

"You know how to drive this thing?"

"I'm fixing to learn." Lorie took the side rail of the gurney and started wheeling Dad back the way they'd come.

Matt and Vincent ran down to the basement.

The place was abandoned. Watching the indicator light on the elevator, they waited in gun stance where they'd be out of sight of the perp.

The elevator dinged, and the doors slid open. The man in the lab coat stepped out, breathing hard.

"Freeze!"

The man ducked back into the elevator and pushed a button. As the doors began to close, Matt dived in after him. The perp aimed a kick at Matt's hand. The gun flew out a narrow gap in the doors and clattered to the basement floor just as the doors closed.

The perp lunged at Matt as the elevator began to rise. Matt ducked to one side, grabbed the man's arm and slammed his head into the elevator wall with a mighty thud. Before he could regain his balance, Matt got him in a headlock.

"Who paid you? Who's behind this?"

As the man started spewing curses, Matt tightened his chokehold. A gurgling sound made Matt loosen his hold just enough to keep from knocking him unconscious. He wanted him awake for interrogation.

The elevator stopped on the first floor. As the doors opened, Deputy Vincent stood outside, breathing hard, arms braced in gun stance.

"Cuffs!"

The still-winded Vincent stood down and helped Matt cuff the would-be kidnapper.

"Any word as to whether someone's found a sign of a bomb?"

Vincent shrugged. "Can't take chances. We still need to get out of here. Bomb squad's already on the premises."

"My piece still in the basement?"

Vincent pulled Matt's gun from the back of his belt and handed it over.

At Vincent's quizzical look, Matt glanced at the perp. "Long story."

"You're too late." The man's voice held a sneer. "By now, she's gone."

Matt's heart sank. *Lorie!*

Mom had been herded out the doors with the rest of the people in E.R. by the time Lorie maneuvered Dad's gurney back toward the emergency exit. The empty corridors echoed with mindless beeps. Her footsteps on the worn gray tiles sounded like gunshots.

No one remained in E.R. The ambulance that had brought Dad sat by the emergency-room doors, abandoned, its motor still running. As Lorie pushed Dad's gurney through the doors, she scanned the parking lot, looking for Mom, or anyone. How far had they made everyone retreat? Clear to the next county?

If this is a nightmare, I want to wake up now!

No. There they were, two blocks away—white-coated doctors, nurses in scrubs, patients on gurneys, in wheelchairs, some standing about looking as dazed as Lorie felt.

"Don't drive so fast, cupcake. I'm getting seasick."

"Sorry, Dad." Lorie slowed her pace and tried to keep the gurney from running away with her.

As she headed past the ambulance, a hand clamped over her mouth as a strong arm grabbed her around the waist. Lorie struggled and kicked back against her captor as the gurney rolled to the curb and stopped, jolting Dad.

"Hey!" Dad's shout was louder than the hospital's alarm system, but Lorie doubted the hospital evacuees heard it from all their distance away.

She tried to open her mouth to let out a scream of her own when a voice murmured in Lorie's ear. "Come quietly, or your father's dead."

Lorie stilled. A moment later, rough hands threw her into the back of the ambulance and slammed the door. Outside, Dad yelled for help as the engine roared to life. On her hands and knees, Lorie toppled sideways into the gear cabinet as the ambulance careened out of the parking lot. Pain socked the back of her head before the world went black.

Matt raced out the door to see the ambulance disappearing down the road, with a frantic-looking Ben on a gurney beside the curb. He ran to Ben's side.

"Don't worry about me!" Ben waved his hand in the direction of the ambulance. "Get after her. Go. Go!"

Vincent was only two steps behind Matt. He jerked his head at the patrol car, and Matt raced around to the passenger side, barely getting the door closed as it roared to life, lights and siren blaring.

Vincent keyed the unit's radio. "All units, this is unit A-1 in pursuit of a stolen ambulance northbound on First, kidnap victim inside. Suspect likely armed and dangerous. Over."

Units began answering as Dispatch came back, ordering assistance.

Matt's heart pounded like a racehorse. If only he hadn't chased the perp. If only—

I need to pray.

Even though he currently was powerless to do anything physical for Lorie, there was still one thing he *could* do. As the patrol car sped down First Street, blasting through red lights with Vincent leaning on the horn, Matt prayed for Lorie's safety, and that they'd be able to reach her in time.

The patrol car clung to the ambulance like a burr to a hunting dog. Vehicles that had pulled over to the right went by in a blur. Matt grasped the armrest, leaning forward as if by sheer will he could make the car go faster. Meanwhile, his mind was racing with questions. How had they been tracked to the hospital? How had the kidnapper even known they'd survived the crash? The way they'd careened off the mountain, he should have assumed they were dead.

The image of Sam McGee from Search and Rescue radioing their location on ham radio popped into Matt's brain. Of course. The kidnapper must have been monitoring two meters. Ham radio was wonderful, but it was public. Anyone with a shortwave receiver could listen.

"Borrow your cell phone again?"

Vincent nodded without taking his eyes off the road.

Matt reached for it as the ambulance took a left onto Highway 32. He keyed in Frank's personal mobile number.

"Sutherland."

"Sheriff, it's MacGregor. Lorie's been kidnapped. Lanier County Deputy Vincent and I are in pursuit of an ambulance headed on Hwy 32 toward Dainger County."

"Roger. We'll set up a roadblock." The phone double-beeped as Frank ended the call.

As the patrol car raced after the ambulance, a semi hauling a load of chickens pulled onto the highway from a crossroad in front of them. The ambulance swerved around, but its driver regained control. Vincent spun the wheel, leaning on the horn again, but the semi's driver lost control. The truck skidded across the road and the trailerload of chicken cages fell onto its side, taking the semi's cab with it. The radio that prevented the driver from hearing their sirens still pounded a heavy-metal beat into the air.

Matt braced himself for impact, but Vincent stomped on the brakes. Tires screamed in protest as they skidded to a halt, inches away from the mountain of poultry.

Matt pounded the dashboard as he watched the ambulance race away, taking Lorie with it.

If it would have helped, Matt would have torn his hair out, especially as the next few minutes passed and he received word that the ambulance had disappeared without ever crossing the roadblock into Dainger County. It could be anywhere. The driver could be clear out of Arkansas into Oklahoma by now.

Returning to the hospital felt like the wrong thing to do, but after the Highway Patrol arrived to help clear the road of dead and dying chickens and round up the living escapees, Deputy Vincent received the call from his dispatcher to return at once.

Anxiety twisted at Matt's guts. Scriptures tried to surface in his brain, telling him not to fret, that God was in charge, but worry kept worming its way to the top. Lorie could be dead by now. The bomb might have gone off at the hospital, injuring her parents and everyone else in a three-block radius. How would he ever explain abandoning them to Lorie if anything happened to them? If only Lorie were alive to explain anything to—

As the patrol car neared the hospital, Matt noticed people reentering the building. A couple of police officers were leading the handcuffed kidnapper out and sticking him into a patrol car. Before Vincent had the car parked, Matt leaped out of it with a terse "Thanks."

Matt raced to the police car, badge already in hand. "MacGregor, Dainger County Sheriff's Department. I need to question this guy."

"Get in line."

Frustration reared its ugly head. Even though he understood the protocol, at times like these he wished he could ignore chain of command. He'd give a great deal to get information out of this guy.

"You'll need to phone Sheriff Sutherland and get him in the loop on this." Matt didn't make it a question, and to his relief, the police officer nodded.

As they drove away, Matt scanned the crowd and spotted Margaret and Ben talking with another Campbelltown police officer. He ran to the gurney where Ben sat, Margaret holding his hand.

"Where's Lorie?" Margaret's hopeful expression made Matt's heart sink like a stone.

"We'll find her."

Ben squeezed Margaret's hand as her face crumpled with grief. "We need to pray, honey."

"What do you think I've been doing?" Margaret sounded as if she'd been stretched past her limit and had finally broken.

"When the situation is desperate is not the time to stop praying, sweetheart."

Ben's words soaked into Matt's heart.

The E.R. doctor joined the city policemen at their side.

"I don't have to stay overnight, do I?" Ben looked hopeful, despite his obvious pain.

"No, you can go home, but I want you to see your own doctor tomorrow." He handed Margaret an oversize file folder. "The X-rays are in there, and he can call for any further information."

As the Narramores were thanking him, a car from the rental agency Matt had called earlier pulled up.

"Matthew MacGregor?"

"Here."

Matt took the keys from the driver, a kid who looked barely old enough to have a license. Matt signed the paperwork, and then helped the Narramores into the car.

As they headed north toward Hwy 32, Matt glanced at Ben, carefully strapped into the front seat next to him. "Can you get a signal on your phone?"

"Margaret, do you have it?"

"Right here."

"Please call the ranch and let them know we're on our way. I've already spoken with Sheriff Sutherland." Matt recited the number.

Margaret nodded and began dialing.

Ben turned his head to look at Matt, letting out a stifled groan. "Aren't we going after Lorie?"

"I'm going after Lorie, but I'll need reinforcements."

"We can help."

Matt sensed Ben's frustration. "I know, but you're a wounded warrior. The best thing you and Margaret can do is pray. Pray we find her. Pray she's all right."

Ben sighed. "That's my little girl. This is killing me."

How could Matt reassure Ben, when he needed his own reassurance? He kept to the speed limit, wishing he had his portable light and siren. Being stopped for a ticket wouldn't get him to Lorie any faster.

Lord, please keep her safe. And let us find her before it's too late.

NINETEEN

Lorie's head was going to explode. Unless she died of being bounced to pieces first. Opening her eyes a tiny crack, she saw an oxygen tank attached to a wall. Oxygen tank?

Memory came flooding back. She'd been thrown into the back of an ambulance. She ran through a mental checklist of who else might be in danger. Dad? On a gurney, probably safe. Mom? Most likely with the rest of the people evacuated from the hospital. Matt? She'd last seen him running after Dad's attacker. Did he know she'd been taken? Was he following her? Or simply wondering where she was?

Lord, please protect them and bring us safely back together. If I'm going to die, Lord, please keep them safe.

Fear threatened to choke her. No. She wasn't going to give way to her situation. God was in charge. He would help her be strong. And she needed all the strength she could get, since no matter what happened, she wasn't going to give in without a fight.

The ambulance jolted to a stop. A traffic light?

The rumble of the engine died.

They'd reached their destination. Lorie scrambled to a standing position and looked for anything she could use as a weapon.

The ambulance shook a little as the driver jumped out.

"I know he wants you, but there's no reason why you and I can't have a little fun first," she heard the man say. The handle turned. A second later, Lorie's kidnapper yanked open the door.

Lorie saw the gun and let loose a stream of foam from the fire extinguisher. She aimed it at his face, and he choked. Gasping for air, he dropped the gun.

Lorie leaped out of the patient compartment, nearly spraining her ankle, and raced past the man, carrying the fire extinguisher with her. He'd left the driver's-side door open, and she jumped inside, ignoring the nick from the scalpel she'd put in her pocket as she tossed the extinguisher on the passenger's seat and started the engine. Lorie slammed the door as her kidnapper grabbed at the handle, wiping foam from his eyes.

The miserable excuse for a road had no place to turn. Lorie drove straight on into the woods, aware that the path could peter out at any moment. Behind her, the man's shouts grew fainter as she put as much distance between them as she could.

The pines towered over the road, so thick that Lorie couldn't determine the direction of the sun. She glanced at her watch. Unbelievable that it was still morning after so much had happened. The sun should be in the east still, if she could ever see past the trees.

The radio crackled, but, aware that radios had probably betrayed their position to the kidnapper, Lorie ignored it. If she called in her position, her tormentor might find her before the authorities did.

All that mattered was getting safely back to Matt and her parents.

Lord, You've gotten me this far. Please get me safely home. And please let this be over soon.

When Matt drove through the gates of Rob Roy Ranch, he found the troops already assembling. The sheriff walked up to the car and opened the doors for Ben and Margaret.

"We're working with Lanier County Sheriff's Department and the Arkansas Highway Patrol. I also alerted the prayer chain at church."

"Oh, thank you!"

Frank helped Ben out of the car as Matt joined his brothers and sisters by the Search and Rescue horses. Sandy held his favorite riding boots. Alana had his hiking boots. Good thinking. His Sunday shoes certainly hadn't helped when they were trying to escape on Chastain Mountain.

Jim looked down from the saddle atop his usual horse, Trailblazer. "How long has it been?"

Matt glanced at his watch. "Nearly three hours. Her folks are frantic, but trying not to show it."

"You riding or driving?" Jake held out the reins of Lightning.

Which should he do? Driving was a lot faster, but if Lorie were being held in a stretch of wilderness, riding could take him where a Jeep couldn't go.

Frank strode over to their position. "Just got word from LCSD. One of their deputies found tracks where the ambulance may have left the highway. They're going in to check now."

"You have the coordinates?"

"It's on the county line, so they'll probably cross into our jurisdiction close to Fiddler's Knob."

By car, that was half an hour or so southeast of the ranch. "I'll drive." Matt took the hiking boots and headed toward one of the ranch's Jeeps.

"Matt, wait up." Frank caught up to him as he had one hand on the door. "There's news about the cartel Grayson Carl ran. San Diego P.D. and the DEA believe that they have rounded up the rest of the major players in California. The chances of Lorie's kidnappers being from there are very slim."

The news socked Matt in the gut. "Then we're back to square one figuring out who's behind this."

"Not necessarily. We've been following an anonymous tip about the drug smuggling. This source refused to give her name, but she sent names, dates, places—it all ties in with somebody we've already had our eye on."

"Adderson?"

Frank shook his head. "Not this time." He handed Matt a photograph of a man stuffing drugs into the wheel well of a car. The auto body shop looked familiar. It should. He'd had his F-150's tune-up done there a month or two ago.

The Pitt Stop.

A chill ran down Matt's spine. "She's sure?"

"Very. And you're not going to believe what else she told me." Frank held out a sheaf of printouts. "Look at this."

Matt stared at the papers. On top was a birth certificate for Grayson Carl, only it called him Grayson Carlos. Born in Colombia in 1970, mother Celia Ortiz y Cabezón. Father—could it be?—José Pitt, attaché to the U.S. Embassy in Bogotá. He raised unbelieving eyes to the sheriff's face.

"Joseph Pitt?"

Frank nodded. "We've been busy tracking things down. Turns out Pitt did a stint in Foreign Service, in Colombia, in the late sixties and early seventies. He was married to a Colombian woman who was killed in the riots in 1974, right before he returned to the States."

"Leaving a son behind?"

"That's the odd part. We're still trying to piece everything together, but it looks very much like Lorie Narramore shot and killed Supervisor Pitt's firstborn son."

Lorie came to a fork in the trail and stepped on the brakes. One branch meandered down, the other up.

"Now what?"

The engine hummed but offered no opinion.

Up? Or down?

Up might lead to the top of a mountain. Down might end at a creek.

"Up it is." *At least if it ends on top of a mountain, I can get my bearings, if there's a clearing.*

Easing off the brakes, Lorie steered in the direction of the upper trail. The ambulance wasn't happy with the rutted dirt and rocks. At times, she slowed to a crawl, always listening for the sound of any vehicle in pursuit. Nothing.

Birdsong filled the air as she edged up the mountain. She could almost enjoy this little adventure, if she weren't so concerned about Mom and Dad. And Matt. Somehow, she had to get back to civilization so she could let Matt know it didn't matter *what* he did for a living. Not anymore.

The dirt trail began to level out a bit as Lorie spotted a fancy log cabin perched on the edge of a clearing. The view it overlooked took Lorie's breath away. Down below, she could see a campground, and, not much farther, a small town. A flash of recognition made her smile. Jen had been telling her about the annual music festival that started at Fiddler's Knob a few years back.

Time enough for that. Seeing a Range Rover parked next to the cabin, Lorie stopped the ambulance and turned off the motor. Maybe the owners would have a cell phone she could use, to let everyone know she'd escaped.

As she approached the front door, it opened.

"Hello. I'm lost. Could I borrow a phone?"

The man filling the door frame moved into the daylight. Recognizing him, Lorie relaxed.

"Oh, Supervisor Pitt. I'm so glad to see you. You won't believe what I've been through."

"Well, good afternoon, Miss Narramore." Supervisor Pitt smiled. "I've been expecting you. Won't you come in?"

The hand he waved at the door held a gun. Lorie blinked, but the gun was still there when she opened her eyes.

"I don't understand."

"I know you don't. You've been very obtuse, but you're about to be enlightened. Do come in." His voice hardened. "Now."

* * *

Matt took the back road to Fiddler's Knob. Frank's information about Joseph Pitt's property included a cabin up on the Knob.

He prayed silently as he drove. His heart convicted him as he thought about Lorie, *his* Lorie. He couldn't stand the thought of losing her…which made his thoughts turn to Owen and Lorene. He'd been so curt with the man, even knowing how he was suffering, how Lorene was suffering. Would it kill him to make peace before she died?

"Forgive me for being a hypocrite, Lord. I told Lorie she needed to forgive people, and here I am still carrying this load of hatred and hurt around."

Matt almost drove past the half-hidden trail up Fiddler's Knob, but turned at the last second, the Jeep's tires kicking up dust.

"All right. I *will* to forgive Owen and Lorene, Lord. I trust You to bring my thoughts into the right place. Please help me to make peace with them before she dies."

A subtle shifting in his being settled peace in his heart, giving him a feeling of lightness that made him aware of just how heavily that angry load had been weighing him down. He should have forgiven them years ago. An image of Lorie's sweet face rose up before him, and with it, a blinding flash of truth. Now he was free to love her. But first, he had to rescue her.

He drove on until he was within a quarter mile of Pitt's cabin and stopped. He'd go the rest of the way on foot, so as not to alert anyone to his presence. After swapping his Sunday shoes for the hiking boots, Matt checked the clip in his handgun. Only three bullets missing. Quickly he reloaded the clip, then replaced the Colt in the shoulder holster and buttoned his jacket. Silently, he swung the rifle by its sling over his shoulder.

Lord, be with us.

* * *

The interior of Supervisor Pitt's cabin was a surprise. The living room reminded her of the lodge on Rob Roy Ranch, but the kitchen was a mass of drug-manufacturing equipment.

This must be the meth lab Matt had been seeking.

Pitt's son Quentin, whom Lorie had seen a few times at the library, looked around, glared at her, sniffed and returned to his work. The bandage on his arm was dark with dried blood. Had he been the one who shot at her on Chastain Mountain? And maybe at her house? All the evidence seemed to point in that direction.

"Have a seat, Miss Narramore." Joseph Pitt waved the gun at a sofa.

Lorie sank onto the edge of the cushion as Pitt walked over to stand in front of a massive fireplace.

"I'm sure you must have questions. Feel free to ask. Anything you like."

Lorie stared at him, taking in the hardness of his face, the coldness of his eyes.

"No questions? What an unusual woman you are." Pitt set the gun on top of the mantelpiece. "Very well. I'll enlighten you on my own. It's important that you understand what you've done—and why you must be held accountable." His fingers stroked a stuffed pheasant that seemed to glower at Lorie with one beady glass eye.

"You still don't know how you angered me in killing Grayson Carl."

Lorie held her breath. Was the supervisor somehow connected to Carl?

"Or, I *should* say, Grayson Carl Pitt."

Lorie's blood turned to ice. "He wasn't—?"

"My son? Oh, yes."

Questions whirled in Lorie's brain, caught in a vortex. How? Why? She could barely recognize one before another blurred by.

"But you helped get me my job here."

Pitt smiled again as he petted the dead pheasant. "And why not? It brought you closer to me. It was much harder, running the intimidation campaign with you sixteen hundred miles away. Gray's people wanted to eliminate you themselves, but with all the trouble they were having with the DEA by then, I talked them out of it. Family, you know. Still important to some people."

Lorie glanced around the living room. A Nazi symbol had been superimposed onto the Stars and Stripes, the white circle with its swastika taking the place of the stars in the blue upper quadrant. So. That was why he had wanted the library to order those books.

"You're an Aryan. How did you explain the existence of your mixed-blood son?"

Pitt's face darkened. She'd hit a nerve.

"I was young and foolish when I was a Foreign Service officer. I hadn't yet embraced the teachings of supremacy. Everyone in the movement knows what I stand for now. They believe me when I say that that's all in the past."

"I believed you. I believed in you." Lorie's heart thudded, pulse pounding in her ears.

"Yes. It's really too bad about you. I think you might have been useful to me."

"So what are you planning now?"

"I've been considering that. You made me suffer a great deal."

"I'm sorry."

"Oh, you're sorry, are you? You murder my son and then you say you're *sorry?*"

"It was self-defense."

"Enough!"

Lorie jumped in spite of herself. She had to *do* something before these evil men could carry out their plans, whatever they were. The only trouble was, she had no earthly idea what to do.

* * *

Matt crept up on the cabin. He'd smelled meth cooking the moment he'd left the Jeep and radioed Frank requesting backup. Maybe this was the break in the case they'd needed. If only it wasn't too late for Lorie.

The ambulance was parked next to a late model black Range Rover. Lorie was here. She had to be. Matt had no doubt he was seriously outnumbered.

Where were the troops? He couldn't wait forever, not with Lorie trapped inside with her kidnappers. The front door was easily accessible, and he could find cover in the trees. The back door led out onto a deck overlooking a meadow.

Moving far enough away from the cabin that he wouldn't be overheard, Matt activated his radio again. "MacGregor. I've found the ambulance at Pitt's cabin. I need that backup, now."

The radio crackled. The sheriff answered. "We have units en route. Hold your position, Mac."

"Roger."

Waiting might very well be the hardest thing he'd ever had to do.

It was amazing, really. Supervisor Pitt didn't look like a madman or a sociopath. Perhaps he had some other mental condition. More likely it was a spiritual condition. Regardless, Lorie knew that she needed to get away from him as soon as possible. She continued to pray silently as she waited for the right moment to act.

"I had great hopes for Gray."

Quentin turned around in the kitchen and gave his father an ugly look, but Pitt's back was to him.

Maybe she could turn Quentin against Pitt.

First, she'd have to keep him talking. "How did you discover you had a son in Colombia?"

"My son found me. Amazing, really. Such a simple

thing. He had finally found his birth records. By then his grandparents were dead. He'd inherited some interesting property, and knew exactly what to do with it. Coffee. Emeralds. Cocaine. He'd become a very clever businessman. Relocating to the United States was a brilliant move on his part. After that, he hired private investigators to locate me, and keep it quiet."

Quentin gave his father another insolent look, which the supervisor missed.

"Why did he keep it a secret? I'd have thought he'd be thrilled to find his father alive after—how long?"

"Thirty-three years. It was—an adjustment, for both of us."

In the kitchen, Quentin made an odd noise and muttered something under his breath.

Clearly this was a sensitive subject. Lorie racked her brain for something that might get an even stronger reaction. "It sounds like he was everything you could want in a son."

Pitt's face hardened. "He was that and more. Until you deliberately stole him from me."

Oops. Wrong move. And this was one chess game that could get her killed. What could she say to derail some of the anger? He seemed proud of how cunning his son had been—maybe that was a good angle to take?

"He had everyone in San Diego convinced he was a true philanthropist."

"But he was, my dear." Pitt smiled at her. "Just as I am. You can check the lists of all the charitable foundations to which I contribute."

Lorie bit her lip. This was getting her no closer to dividing and conquering. How could she twist the knife for Quentin without setting off his father?

"I can't understand why you're willing to risk everything you love. You've already lost one son. Surely you don't want to lose your other one."

"And why would I do that? Quentin isn't going any-where, are you, boy?"

Quentin walked in from the kitchen. "Doesn't look much like it. You, on the other hand, have been a peck of trouble from the get-go, Ms. Librarian. We should have just killed you. But no." He glanced at his father. *"He* had to drag it out, to make you suffer."

"Now, now, Quentin. You know I didn't mean for you to get shot. Running them off the road should have finished the whole family. If you'd done a better job—"

Quentin turned purple. "I suppose you think your *brilliant* son Gray could have done a better job." He swore. "Your pet project here shot him while he was trying to off that double-crossing chick who was going to turn him in. He couldn't even protect himself, let alone his operation. And now you're so smart, you've probably screwed up our own operation with your stupid vendetta!"

"Shut up, Quent. It's over. We'll take Miss Narramore to the old Cooper place and set it on fire. All the evidence will point to Adderson, and we'll be home free."

Pitt gestured with the gun. "All right, Miss Narramore. Time to go. If you're good, I may even shoot you before I set the place on fire."

Lord, you were with Shadrach, Meshach and Abednego in the midst of the fire, but please—

"Get the door, Quent."

Collecting a rope from the hall tree, Quentin put it over his shoulder and opened the door.

"After you, Ms. Narramore."

With no choice but to follow, Lorie headed toward her doom.

TWENTY

As Matt watched, the door opened and Lorie walked outside, followed by Supervisor Pitt carrying a semiautomatic pistol aimed at the small of her back. Pitt's son Quentin trailed after them, a rope slung carelessly over his left shoulder.

From his position behind a pine ten yards away, Matt lifted the rifle and sighted through it. He'd take out the supervisor first, and then worry about his son. Pitt's proximity to Lorie made this tricky. If he missed…

He couldn't miss. Lorie's life depended on it.

Very gently, he started to squeeze the trigger—

Cold metal pressed against his right temple. Glancing at the man who had the drop on him, Matt recognized him as Paulie Jones, one of the mechanics who worked at the Pitt Stop.

"Nuh-uh. Lower that rifle nice and slow."

If he complied, he and Lorie were both dead. If he didn't, he and Lorie were both dead.

Lord, help!

Matt eased the rifle down from his shoulder and held it out to one side. It was ripped from his grasp and tossed into a tangle of brambles. As Jones fumbled at Matt's holster, Matt reached up and grabbed the mechanic's gun hand, forcing it upward. It discharged, the bullet slamming into a pine branch.

As they struggled over the gun, it went off again, the bullet flying wildly to hit Quentin Pitt in the ankle. He went down, squealing like a wounded razorback.

"Daddy!"

"Shut up, Quent."

Jones seemed to have superhuman strength. He fought like a madman.

Dimly, Matt heard Lorie shout. "Meth!"

Now he understood. If Jones were on meth, he'd have enhanced reflexes, and enough chemicals pumping through his brain to make him think he could conquer the world. Matt prayed as he fought, prayed for the strength to overcome the addictive drug that had fueled the blitzkrieg.

Matt wrestled the gun from Jones and smacked it into his temple, felling him. Jones lay flat on the ground, unconscious.

"Stop right there!"

Matt wheeled in the direction of Pitt's shout, going into a gun crouch. The supervisor had Lorie in a chokehold, pistol to her head.

"Throw the gun down or she dies right now!"

Matt shook his head. "You'll kill her anyway. That's always been your plan."

Pitt raised an eyebrow. "Don't be a fool, Deputy. I can make you rich."

Matt spat on the ground. "I don't need your money."

He loved her, and at any second, he might lose her. And she was…reaching into her pocket? *What's Lorie doing?*

"I can give you power!"

"I have God's power on my side."

"God!" Pitt sneered. "You think God cares what happens to any of us?" He shook his head. "You waited too long, Deputy. Tell your girlfriend goodbye."

As Pitt's finger slowly tightened on the trigger, Lorie's hand flew up, sunlight glinting off a deadly looking scalpel. Pitt screamed in pain as the gun flew out of his hand, blood pouring from his slashed fingers.

"Down!" Matt shouted.

Lorie dived toward the ground, rolling away from her captors.

Matt pulled the trigger.

Pitt reeled backward, blood spurting from his chest before he hit the ground.

Quentin screamed. "Daddy!" Despite his injured ankle and bandaged arm, he reached for the gun his father had dropped. Matt shot it out of reach. "Don't move, Junior."

Lorie scrambled to her feet and hurried over to Supervisor Pitt, looking around for anything she could use to stop the bleeding. Kneeling beside him, she bunched up her skirt and pressed it onto his chest.

Pitt's eyes opened. "What—what're you doing?"

"Trying to save your life."

Pitt blinked. "Why?"

"Because I couldn't save your son's." She pressed harder, but blood soaked her skirt and stained her hands.

Pitt blinked, seeming to try to focus on Lorie's face.

"You—forgive me?"

Matt couldn't stand it one more second. "Lorie, get away from him!"

She turned to look at Matt and shook her head. "No. I have to do this." She looked back at the man who lay there, slowly dying under her hands, despite her best efforts.

"Yes. I forgive you."

Matt's hands clenched the pistol, ready to fire again if necessary. Standing there, watching, not knowing what to do or how to pray, Matt remembered the scripture, and let the Holy Spirit intercede on their behalf.

Pitt drew a gurgling breath. Maybe he planned to use it to forgive her for her role in Grayson's death. Or to apologize for what he'd done. They'd never know for sure—that breath was his last.

"Daddy! No!" Quentin's cry of anguish rent the pine-scented air.

Lorie stood up as the sound of sirens penetrated the woods. Tears poured down her face. Still covered in pine tar from yesterday, and now drenched in blood, she should have looked a wreck.

She was beautiful.

"Get the rope, Lorie."

Picking it up from where Quentin had dropped it, Lorie brought it to Matt.

"You any good with knots?"

She nodded, her tangled hair flopping around her face.

"Tie up Jones."

Lorie knelt in the dirt and, with moves that would make any bulldogger proud, bound Jones hand and foot while Matt kept his gun trained on Quentin.

After she hog-tied the mechanic, Lorie returned to Matt's side. He gathered her to himself with his free arm as the cavalry arrived.

"I don't care if you're in law enforcement, Matt."

"And I don't care that your name is Lorie."

After a Lanier County and two Dainger County Sheriff's Department SUVs drove into the clearing to take charge of the situation, Matt handed off the gun to Gerhardt so he could pull Lorie into a better hug.

"I love you, Lorie Narramore."

She blinked away tears. "And I love you, *Deputy* Matt."

When Matt's lips met Lorie's, he knew it was true. She *did* love him. Everything was going to be all right.

EPILOGUE

Lorie sat by Matt's side in the living room of the family house on Rob Roy Ranch, surrounded by her family, Matt's family and the Sutherlands. Vangie Rae hadn't aged a day since the last time Lorie'd seen her—the glamour industry had been able to accomplish that much. Still as slim as she'd been in high school, Vangie was now twice as blonde, and even bubblier in person than she was on the phone, despite the mixed feelings at tonight's get-together.

"It's a pity Joseph Pitt didn't live to stand trial." Frank Sutherland wore the same look of concern Lorie had come to know and understand. What a hard job he had. She was glad Matt was only a lowly deputy, on his way to becoming a detective. Maybe Frank *needed* a wife like Vangie Rae, to add some lightness to his life and keep him sane.

"Now, Frank. The county will have quite enough to deal with giving Quentin, Jones and the rest of Pitt's crew fair trials. Probably have to have a change of venue." Matt looked as though he was glad about that.

"So Grayson Carl was Joseph Pitt's son." Dad shook his head. "I'd heard the drug ring in Dainger County was widespread, but I had no idea it had links to Colombia."

Lorie linked fingers with Matt. "And I had no idea Carl had ties to Dainger County."

"I bet you'd never have come back if you'd known, and then look at what you'd have missed!" Vangie beamed at

Lorie. "And was I right, or was I right about the handsome Deputy MacGregor?"

Lorie blushed. "Now, Vangie, nothing's settled."

"Not yet," Matt said, "but soon. I think we need a little more privacy before I ask Lorie what I want to ask her." He'd told her earlier of making peace with Lorene and Owen, something that touched her heart deeply.

Lorie looked up at him and saw a gleam in his blue eyes. A shiver of pure delight tickled her to the core.

"So does this wrap up your meth-lab investigation?" Dad asked. He was sitting with a hand on Mom's knee, since it hurt his ribs too much to try to put his arm around her.

"I don't think so." Frank leaned back against the sofa cushion. "We're still looking closely at Leonard Adderson. But serving that search warrant on the Pitt Stop showed us how they've been fixing cars to transport drugs. At least that's one thing we'll be able to shut down." Frank's cell phone beeped, and he glanced at the text message. "In fact, someone's just arrived who will be able to clear up a lot of your questions."

A tap at the door sent Sandy to answer it. When Lorie saw who was standing there, her jaw dropped.

"Ms. Montoya!"

The lithe brunette who came into the room looked a bit uncomfortable, but she approached Lorie, who stood to meet her.

"Actually, it isn't Candace Montoya." She reached into the Coach bag at her side and pulled out a leather folder, flipping it open so Lorie could see a badge and ID. "I'm Special Agent Carmen Machada, DEA. I apologize for running out on you and not appearing at the trial, but I was in deep cover. Testifying would have blown an investigation that had been ongoing for three years."

"DEA?" Lorie put a hand to her head. "You didn't just leave me in the lurch, then."

"No." Regret crossed the agent's intelligent face. "I did everything I could to supply information to your attorney and to make sure you weren't convicted. I'm glad it worked."

"So am I."

"I'm happy to say the undercover work paid off. You shouldn't have to worry about the cartel being out to get you anymore, Ms. Narramore."

Relief made Lorie weak in the knees. Matt appeared at her side and wrapped an arm around her shoulders, keeping her upright.

"Thank you. Oh, thank you so much!"

Carmen smiled. "Just doing my job."

Frank spoke up. "Since she helped round up the rest of the Orgulloso cartel's California arm, Ms. Machada has been assigned as liaison to the Dainger County Sheriff's Department. She's going to help us find the rest of our hydra-headed monster."

"Why, isn't that the grandest thing!" Vangie Rae lit up. "You're not married, are you, Miss Carmen?"

Ms. Machada looked startled. "No. Why?"

"Well, there are several handsome deputies I've been trying to match up with someone special—"

"Vangie Rae!" Frank roared, as the room dissolved into laughter.

* * * * *

Dear Reader,

Thank you so much for reading *No Place to Run,* the first of what I hope will be many novels set in my fictional county in beautiful Western Arkansas.

Books don't happen in a vacuum, and that's a good thing! So many things contribute to a story that sometimes it's hard to know where to begin. This one began with a blank page and one sentence during that crazy time of year known as National Novel Writing Month, or NaNoWriMo. Once the note appeared on the page on Lorie's desk, the rest began to take shape.

The book has undergone many changes since its first mad rush of creation, but its message remains the same: love and forgiveness are two essential things in life.

As far as I know, neither the city nor county library systems of San Diego has ever held a charity auction at the Hotel Del Coronado—or anywhere else—and I'm sure I don't have to tell you that the interlibrary loan system has nothing to do with transporting illegal substances! I have the highest regard for not only the library systems and the Hotel Del, but also the Coronado Police Department and San Diego County Sheriff's Department. All of the county's law enforcement agencies, in fact! Lorie's dim view is colored by her experiences, and is in no way intended to make light of the fine work done by the excellent men and women in law enforcement!

If you'd like to know more about Dainger County, please visit www.daingercounty.com. You can write to me at marionlaird@gmail.com, or c/o Love Inspired Books, 233 Broadway, Suite 1001, New York, NY 10279 U.S.A.

May the Lord bless you!

Marion Faith Laird

Questions for Discussion

1. Lorie still feels guilty for having taken a life, even though it was self-defense. Do you think she's right to have this feeling, even though she saved two lives? Why or why not?

2. Matt has had trouble forgiving his ex-fiancée and the friend with whom she betrayed him. Even though he has moved on and thinks he's over the betrayal, it has affected his ability to trust women. Do you think this is a normal reaction, or has Matt carried it too far?

3. Even though Lorie is being threatened, she has trouble trusting anyone in law enforcement. How would you react in her situation?

4. Lorie left San Diego and returned to her roots in Western Arkansas because of the constant harassment after her acquittal. If you were in her situation, would you move or stay and try to fight?

5. Illegal drugs are a problem in Dainger County. Are they a problem where you live? If so, how much of a problem, and how does it affect you personally?

6. Neither Lorie nor Matt wants to be attracted to each other. Are they justified in their reaction? If so, who do you think has the better reason to want to avoid a romance, Lorie or Matt?

7. Supervisor Pitt has a thriving legitimate business and attends a church, and yet he is leading a double life as a drug lord and Nazi sympathizer. Do you think

it is possible for him to make peace with God? Why or why not?

8. In 1974, when Pitt's first wife was killed, Colombia was the scene of much unrest and political turmoil. How much do you think this affected his mental state, to lose his wife, and to believe his son was also dead?

9. When Lorie is recounting the details of her case to Matt, she tells him the woman whose life she saved never showed up at the trial. What effect do you think this had on Lorie?

10. Matt chose to go into law enforcement rather than become a rancher like his brothers. Do you think this was a wise decision or not?

11. When Matt's fiancée dumped him after he refused to turn down his scholarship to the University of Louisville, do you think she was just using that as an excuse? Why or why not?

12. Lorie is constantly forced to face her fears and deal with the harassment and increasing danger. In her situation, would you let fear overcome you, or would you find a way to deal with it? If so, how would you deal with it?

13. Lorie believes she can trust Supervisor Pitt because he helped her get her job. Do you think that Lorie was easily fooled, or was Pitt very good at hiding his true colors?

14. When Lorie regains consciousness in the back of the ambulance, she immediately looks around for some-

thing to use as a weapon. What would you do in her situation? What tools would you choose for your escape?

15. Matt and Lorie each pray as their situation unfolds. Do you think the story would have had the same ending if they had not prayed? Why or why not?

REQUEST YOUR FREE BOOKS!
2 FREE RIVETING INSPIRATIONAL NOVELS PLUS 2 FREE MYSTERY GIFTS

YES! Please send me 2 FREE Love Inspired® Suspense novels and my 2 FREE mystery gifts (gifts are worth about $10). After receiving them, if I don't wish to receive any more books, I can return the shipping statement marked "cancel." If I don't cancel, I will receive 4 brand-new novels every month and be billed just $4.74 per book in the U.S. or $5.24 per book in Canada. That's a savings of at least 21% off the cover price. It's quite a bargain! Shipping and handling is just 50¢ per book in the U.S. and 75¢ per book in Canada.* I understand that accepting the 2 free books and gifts places me under no obligation to buy anything. I can always return a shipment and cancel at any time. Even if I never buy another book, the two free books and gifts are mine to keep forever.

123/323 IDN F5AC

Name _____ (PLEASE PRINT) _____

Address _____ Apt. # _____

City _____ State/Prov. _____ Zip/Postal Code _____

Signature (if under 18, a parent or guardian must sign) _____

Mail to the **Harlequin® Reader Service:**
IN U.S.A.: P.O. Box 1867, Buffalo, NY 14240-1867
IN CANADA: P.O. Box 609, Fort Erie, Ontario L2A 5X3

**Are you a current subscriber to Love Inspired Suspense books and want to receive the larger-print edition?
Call 1-800-873-8635 or visit www.ReaderService.com.**

* Terms and prices subject to change without notice. Prices do not include applicable taxes. Sales tax applicable in N.Y. Canadian residents will be charged applicable taxes. Offer not valid in Quebec. This offer is limited to one order per household. Not valid for current subscribers to Love Inspired Suspense books. All orders subject to credit approval. Credit or debit balances in a customer's account(s) may be offset by any other outstanding balance owed by or to the customer. Please allow 4 to 6 weeks for delivery. Offer available while quantities last.

Your Privacy—The Harlequin® Reader Service is committed to protecting your privacy. Our Privacy Policy is available online at www.ReaderService.com or upon request from the Harlequin Reader Service.
We make a portion of our mailing list available to reputable third parties that offer products we believe may interest you. If you prefer that we not exchange your name with third parties, or if you wish to clarify or modify your communication preferences, please visit us at www.ReaderService.com/consumerschoice or write to us at Harlequin Reader Service Preference Service, P.O. Box 9062, Buffalo, NY 14269. Include your complete name and address.

LIS13R

SPECIAL EXCERPT FROM

Love Inspired

*Join the ranching town of Jasper Gulch, Montana,
as they celebrate 100 years!*

Here's a sneak peek at
HER MONTANA COWBOY
by Valerie Hansen, the first of six books in the
BIG SKY CENTENNIAL *miniseries.*

For the first time in longer than Ryan Travers could re-call, he was having trouble keeping his mind on his work. He couldn't have cared less about Jasper Gulch's missing time capsule; it was pretty Julie Shaw who occupied his thoughts.

"That's not good," he muttered as he stood on a metal rung of the narrow bucking chute. This rangy pinto mare wasn't called Widow-maker for nothing. He could not only picture Julie Shaw as if she were standing right there next to the chute gates, he could imagine her light, uplifting laughter.

Actually, he realized with a start, that *was* what he was hearing. He started to glance over his shoulder, intending to scan the nearby crowd and, hopefully, locate her.

"Clock's ticking, Travers," the chute boss grumbled. "You gonna ride that horse or just look at her?"

Rather than answer with words, Ryan stepped across the top of the chute, raised his free hand over his head and leaned way back. Then he nodded to the gateman.

The latch clicked.

The mare leaped.

Ryan didn't attempt to do anything but ride until he heard the horn blast announcing his success. Then he straightened as best he could and worked his fingers loose with his free hand while pickup men maneuvered close enough to help him dismount.

To Ryan's delight, Julie Shaw and a few others he recognized from before were watching. They had parked a flatbed farm truck near the fence beside the grandstand and were watching from secure perches in its bed.

Julie had both arms raised and was still cheering so wildly she almost knocked her hat off. "Woo-hoo! Good ride, cowboy!"

Ryan's "Thanks" was swallowed up in the overall din from the rodeo fans. Clearly, Julie wasn't the only spectator who had been favorably impressed.

He knew he should immediately report to the area behind the strip chutes and pick up his rigging. And he would. In a few minutes. As soon as he'd spoken to his newest fan.

Don't miss the romance between Julie and rodeo hero Ryan in HER MONTANA COWBOY by Valerie Hansen, available July 2014 from Love Inspired®.

FLOOD ZONE

by

DANA MENTINK

Mia Sandoval's friend is murdered under mysterious circumstances—and the single mother is a suspect. Her only ally is a man she isn't sure she can trust. Search-and-rescue worker Dallas Black has a past as harrowing as Mia's own, and the police are suspicious of them both. With no choice but to work with secretive Dallas, Mia discovers he's as complicated as the murder they're forced to investigate to clear her name. Yet as a flood ravages their small Colorado town, a killer is determined that Mia, Dallas and their evidence get swept away to a watery grave.

Stormswept

Finding true love in the midst of nature's fury

Available July 2014 wherever
Love Inspired books and ebooks are sold.

Find us on Facebook at
www.Facebook.com/LoveInspiredBooks

LI44608